Shang My Love

A Road To A Gentler World

•

Author: A. N. "Shen" Sengupta
Editing by: Author, Arati Sengupta, Dr. Jharna Chatterjee, Narayan
Sengupta
Cover Design: Author and Shomit N. Sengupta
Author's photo: Arati Sengupta
Published by Asit Narayan Sengupta in as both a paperback and as an e. book

First Published: May 2013 as an e. book through Amazon's Kindle Direct Publisher and in May 2013 in paperback through Createspace

ISBN-13: 978-1489554321
ISBN-10: 1489554327
BISAC: Fiction/General

Dedication

To my exemplary Parents, Elders and Teachers, who guided me through my formative years.

Introduction to Part 1

I often wonder if we can ever comprehend the enormity of the gift of Life, which is so very precious that words can in no way even hint at its true meaning. Imagine, it exists nowhere else in the eternity of the Universe. Contemplate how unique we are to be endowed with this priceless gift. And ponder how mindlessly we squander it away in so many self-destructive ways. There have been several responses proposed to solve this dilemma, but some relate to only selected aspects of life, and others advocate the use of slave labor or that of genetically created sub-humans to enable creation of an equitable society. Some propose to use behavioral engineering to simply change people so that they pursue noble causes.

This book is a humble attempt to urge people to appreciate the uniqueness of Life and go from there. It attempts to deal with all aspects of today's world, with an eye toward the future, while always focusing on the utmost preciousness of Life. Nothing more and nothing less. The proposals shun all extremes or anything contrived. They are highly realizable, cost-effective and most humane. Also they are woven with a love story, partly to demonstrate that the proposed changes can be brought about through gentle means and not remotely through any coercion.

There is no intention whatsoever to bring into the discussion any specific country, people, social custom, belief and such. Coincidence, if any, is unintentional.

The book talks about Shangri-La, a country, which with all its uniqueness, is assumed to exist. The question remains how more Shangri-Las can come into being, given the fact that the world is very different in reality.

Introduction to Part 2

Part 2 of the book proposes a way to make most countries of the world, if not all, like Shangri-Las, where Life is valued above all and everything else gently flows from there.

Table of Contents

Part 1

Chapter 1. Ryan at Home

Ryan Lee-Roy Cameronsky, a well-built and handsome man in his mid- thirties, is truly an international person. His name is an image of his heritage. He has many different bloods: Hispanic, Chinese, Indian and European, including Russian. This is not unlike the mix which has been rather common in a few countries since long. He does not know all the details of his genealogy and he does not really care. In the world he lives, it has become rather common to have "melting" of all kinds. Since people do not care to spell out their long mixed-heritage names and he is also tired of doing so time and again, and having his name mispronounced, he introduces himself simply as Ryan. He is perfectly happy with it. What matters most is that his ancestry is firmly based in developed countries, whose progress is measured by their respective "gross domestic products" or GDPs.

Presently he lives in a developed country, where he was born of a highly successful businessman father and a well-educated and charming mother. He has lived occasionally in other countries, but always in a developed country, which routinely provides common conveniences and facilities, and lots of it. He himself as well as his two younger siblings, a brother and a sister, grew up in what one might call a life of luxury and always had more than they could possibly use or keep count of. Their big mansion had ten bedrooms, as many bathrooms, a living room which was so large that it could easily hold one hundred people for a party, and of course there was a good-size indoor swimming pool. And there was a six-car garage. Theirs was not unique in the neighborhood. In every activity in which the family was involved, abundance was the rule. All three siblings went to Ivy-League schools for both their undergraduate and graduate years, and received prestigious degrees in finance and law. All of them became successful corporate executives, made good money, were happily married, owned lavish homes in golf-course communities, and were highly regarded in their respective communities, for their services.

Common sense told that Ryan should have been a happy person, and on the surface, he was. Yet Ryan often felt that something was missing. Was it all too good to be true? Was having everything one would normally wish to have, so easily, since day one of his life, made him paradoxically unhappy and restless? As he wrestled with his own mind, he slowly realized that having everything within easy reach, without having to earn it, and so much for which he had no real use, had progressively blunted his sense of appreciating and treasuring what he had. To him anything was easily dispensable, including even people. Nothing seemed to be permanent.

Ryan had a wonderful wife. Her background was not unlike his. She was his school-sweetheart and an equal partner in his life. To their common friends they made a very attractive and ideal couple. Yet in one key aspect they were unlike each other. She was perfectly contented with her life as it was, and cherished all her possessions, all the good life, the endless parties, and the subtle competitions between the ladies for the best fashions. Above all, she had a good husband. Ryan loved his wife but could not connect too well with all the material wealth, which they happened to have. The natural outcome was conflict. Initially they both laughed it away and their affection for each other won the day. But progressively the paths of their minds diverged, and went in their own separate ways. After several years of putting up a brave face to the impending inevitability, they decided to part from each other but remain friends nonetheless. Instead of having a bitter divorce battle they promised to remain helpful friends forever.

Breakup of the marriage made him no happier than before. But it did not break him down either. In a way he missed the life he had gotten used to, and yet there was a feeling of relief from an undefinable burden on his mind. Since he and his estranged wife had to share their material possessions there was a bit of pinch, but nothing truly appreciable. The major difference would be the loss of some common friends, who felt uneasy with sharing their happily-married lives with two very attractive singles. Since the divorce was based on divergence of minds and not adultery, cruelty, financial problems or the like, Ryan did not want to contest the possession of their house. He let his estranged wife continue to live there. To be honest, he welcomed the opportunity of being away from his material possessions for the benefit of being a part of the wide world. He decided that he would take a break from the life he had inherited and see for himself if he could find out what made his mind restless in the midst of plenty. His solo journey began in earnest.

First he bought a condominium in a secure location in a high-rise building overlooking a great view. Once somewhat settled in his new habitat and a new life as a single, he bought a small recreational vehicle (RV). The choice of a small one was deliberate. It contrasted with the large home he had voluntarily given up. He now started traveling earnestly. Even though he could afford to travel by air easily, he purposely chose to do otherwise so that he would have maximum flexibility as to where he wanted to go, where he would spend the nights and how long he would drive at a stretch. He felt that this way he could be in touch with diverse people and have the opportunity of spending some real time with them. An added bonus would be the opportunity to spend more time with nature, instead of the familiar manicured golf-course. He was very pleased with his decisions, for almost intuitively he felt that all this might help him find the reason for the restlessness in his mind.

At his first stop in a very posh area, where one had to pay a hefty reservation fee, he got a space next to a sea-shore by a mountain. Here he met several couples and singles and spent time with them going for hikes, preparing food on an outdoor grill, having dinner together in one R.V. or another, and weather permitting, even under the canopy of the sky. They swam, sailed, canoed, played board-games or simply chit-chatted about everything that one could think of. To his surprise, he found out that the restless feeling he personally had amidst plenty was shared by many others. The stated reasons varied widely but no one could be truly sure. Quite a few were concerned about global warming and its rather visible consequences such as widespread flooding, widespread drought, diminishing forest cover, rising sea-levels and the like, even though they could not make direct cause-and-effect connections. Others were concerned about a long list of more immediate issues, such as sprawl, the ever-growing concrete-spread and traffic grid-locks, aging infrastructure and cost of maintenance, and also pre-marital sex, violence and profanity portrayed on TV, rising crime, corruption and what not. Globalization, together with instant communication, had evidently made things highly volatile. It used to be that when a super-power would sneeze other countries would catch pneumonia. But now, even when a tiny country anywhere in the world would have a slight cold the giants would catch a bad flu. Quite a few were having marital problems. And others had health issues to deal with. Some were noticeably worried about the future of their children and grand-children. He soon realized that the real and perceived problems were too numerous and that grass was not necessarily greener on the other bank. To find out more about why people felt restless he continued his journey.

Next he stopped deliberately in a park by a lake, which was for people who for most part liked to camp, even though there was a sprinkling of small RVs like his. Thus it was not difficult for him to blend in. Here the people were mostly from the middle class. He mingled with them at every opportunity. Here too, he met both couples and singles, and shared every kind of activity with them. The prevailing issue for feeling restless was impending financial insecurity and not knowing what future held for them. Global problems took a back seat. There was a feeling that while their job-security was at stake and values of their homes were dropping, cost of everything that they needed for life's essentials was rising rapidly, medical expenses were going through the stratosphere and beyond their reach, and the promise of security at old age was fading. They were vaguely aware that while their country's GDP was among the highest in the world, and its percentage was ever growing, they were having an increasingly difficult time in making both ends meet. Though the advent of computerization and instant long-distance communication were to have reduced their workloads, they had little free time. Even on their vacation trips they were carrying their files and work with them, thanks to having laptops, and were on call at all times. Did they have a sense of well-being, he wondered. No one talked about it. Possibly they were so pre-occupied with their fear about their present and future that to think of general well-being would be a luxury.

Ryan moved on. This time he sought out a place where he could meet the have-nots. He could find it easily in a public park on the shore of a river. There was no charge to camp, or park one's vehicle there. It was not too easy to blend in, but he deliberately maintained a very low profile. He parked his RV in a discreet corner and mingled with others as much as he could. To his utter surprise, he met lots of people who had a sense of well-being in spite of having very few material possessions. It was not a case of plain living and high thinking, but more of plain living and plain thinking. They were blissfully unaware of what was going on outside their immediate environment. They knew that they were deprived of the luxuries which were visible to them as they traveled outside their own realm and also through television shows. But it did not really matter. For most part their basic necessities were met: a small house or an apartment, simple food if not the most health-giving, an old car, electricity, clean water, and basic healthcare provided for free or at a nominal cost. Their incomes were modest. So were their needs. They did not have much to lose and no worries about their own future, let alone that of their children or grandchildren. Their best assets were not what mattered to the wealthy or even the middle class, but their equally deprived friends with whom they happily shared what they had, misery and all.

●

Chapter 2. Stranger in Shangri-La

Ryan kept repeating these experiences as often as he could, not only in his own country but in several others that he visited. But he did not find what he was looking for. He could not understand why his mind was always restless, in spite of having all the material possessions in a country with one of the highest gross national products or GDPs. While his wife was happy with it all, he was not. For many years he had been aware of the existence of a strange land. Its name was Shangri-La. It apparently adopted a new kind of measure for well-being, namely, gross national well-being or GNW. No one knew for sure what its GDP was, since it never published it, even if it had this figure. He had heard that the most prominent aspect of this country was that its people were primarily in a state of happiness and general well-being. Could this be true, he wondered. To find it out for himself he decided one day that he would just go there. To reach the gateway to this land was not difficult. But he was not prepared for the experience thereafter. Little did he know that it would change his life forever.

There was no marked border or a built-up gateway to Shangri-La. One travelled a short distance along the plains on a two-lane paved road, with agricultural fields interspersed with groves of fruit trees, on both sides. There were low-rise hillocks ahead in the distance. The road sloped up gradually. It made a sudden turn, and Ryan found himself driving slowly between two hills, forming a green gateway. Presently there was a level piece of land paved with red bricks and with a large fountain in the middle. At the far end there was a small and beautiful kiosk. Inside, there were several young men, who were obviously border attendants. There was a line of colorful flags of the country, on tall masts, on one side of the level space. And there were beautiful flowering trees defining the other side. Ryan stopped his vehicle, got off and walked slowly toward the kiosk.

Simultaneously, two of the attendants emerged and walked toward him. They smiled, welcomed him with folded hands and spoke in crisp English: “Welcome to Shangri-La.” Ryan was surprised that they spoke English and that too so well. He was much more surprised that there was no security or customs checking. But he kept his surprise to himself and said: “Thank you very much. I am a traveler. I have traveled through many countries. I heard of your great country and its belief in well-being as the model of development and came to see it firsthand. Could you please tell me where I could spend a few nights?" One of them replied: "It is no problem, sir. We have many country-inns. They are run by individual families or sometimes a group of families, and if you wish you can have your meals there or outside in the many large and small restaurants. However, our roads are not wide and we discourage using our roads for large and also small gasoline-powered vehicles. You may be prepared to park yours at the inn of your choice, and then switch to an alternate mode of travel, like walking, an electric-bicycle, an electric mini-bus, or an electric train for long distances. Please drive straight ahead about one hundred kilometers and you will reach our capital 'Nondon', where there are many inns, large and small. We know that your stay will be most pleasant." Ryan asked: "I am so surprised that you did not do any security or customs checking. How come?" The young man replied: "Sir, we are pretty good at telling a lot by just looking at one's face and gestures. Also thanks to the new technology available we are able to check a person out, if we feel that we need to.

This is not very different from being able to check one's credit rating instantly. We do not believe in indiscriminate searches. Our policy is to trust unless there is a good reason not to. We have not failed yet. Yours is a very honest face. Your gestures are those of a friend. Enjoy your visit to Shangri-La." Thus reassured Ryan proceeded toward Nondon after exchanging greetings.

He was in no hurry and drove slowly. The road flowed along the contours of the undulating terrain and made gentle turns. There was a belt of large shade trees on either side of the road. Beyond the trees there were frequent patches of farmland, groves of fruit trees and clusters of brightly painted single or two-story homes. A very notable feature was the presence of a solar panel and a wind-turbine on each roof. Farmers, both men and women, in colorful costumes, were working in the fields using small electric tractors and other farm machines and equipment. Narrow roads connected the home-clusters to the main road on which Ryan was traveling. Fellow travelers on the road were on electric bicycles. There were a few cars and occasional mini-buses too, but they were invariably electric. Some of the people had not seen a recreation vehicle before.

They were rather intrigued by its appearance and waved at Ryan with a smile. He happily waved back. The weather was excellent. There were patches of cloud in the sky. The unhurried and friendly atmosphere was almost contagious. Ryan reflected back on his homeland, where everyone drove a gasoline-powered sedan or SUV on four-to-ten lane roads as fast as one could, some even talking or texting on cell-phones and usually carrying no passenger. It was always a mad rush with no time to spare for the places that they were whizzing past. He reflected on the increasing loss of "urban places" and smiled to himself thinking of an article which read something like: "Going there should be half the fun, but when you finally arrive there, there is no there, there."

Today he did not have to rush like his life depended on driving as fast as he could. After about two leisurely hours he arrived in a densely populated settlement with mostly single and two story colorful buildings, huddling together. Here again he noticed solar panels and wind-turbines on all the roofs. As he drove, looking for an inn to rest for the night, he realized that almost no inn faced the road directly. Instead, he found occasional squares, which were surrounded by commercial buildings, including small inns. A relatively large building existed inside some of the squares. He learnt later, that they were used for multiple community purposes. Trees were everywhere in the squares and they were either shade trees or fruit trees. There were also wide pedestrian walks, flower beds, fountains and seating. He stopped in one such square, parked his vehicle in one of the few public parking spaces for vehicles and walked to a nearby inn. Its name was Inn Jasmine. He noticed that all the inns on the square were named after flowers, like Magnolia Inn and Lotus Inn.

Inn Jasmine had a tiny landscaped courtyard in front. There was a place for shoes on one side of the entrance to the inn. As per instructions in English and the local language, Shangri-Lan, he took off his shoes and put on the special canvas slippers reserved for the guests. He entered the tiny but well-furnished lobby, at the far end of which was a counter with a panoramic painting of Nondon on the rear wall. To one side there was a small lounge with comfortable seating, a few board-game tables and a large-screen television set. As his eyes wandered, a young lady in her late-twenties welcomed him with a big smile. She said in a musical voice: "Sir, welcome to our inn. I am Malya or in short, Lya. May I help you?" Ryan replied: "You certainly may. I am Ryan. I am a traveler and I heard of Shangri-La as a land which values people's well-being above all things. So, after visiting many lands, I came to see yours and would like to stay in your inn for a few days." She replied: "Of course. We have a nice room upstairs. It overlooks the square and the inner courtyard-garden. I think that you will like it. Where is your luggage?" Ryan replied: "My bags are in my recreation vehicle, which I have parked in the square." Lya replied: "Please park your vehicle in the rear of the inn. Please do not forget to switch back to your outside shoes when you go out of the inn and change back to the slippers when you return." Ryan did not forget, even though he found this to be a strange custom.

He returned with a few bags and headed for his room. The building was U-shaped around a tiny but carefully nurtured garden, which sported flowing water emitting a soothing sound. The wall enclosing the garden had flowering vines hanging from vases at different levels. By virtue of being indoor, this pocket-sized garden appeared to be larger than it really was. Ryan paused here for a minute or two before going to his room. It was medium-size with a large glazed window overlooking the square but only a bamboo curtain on the courtyard side. The entire floor was covered with carefully woven colorful mats and there were a few pieces of low-rise furniture, but no bed. He soon discovered that a bed was hidden upright in one wall. One would pull it down when needed. There was a wooden counter along the external wall. On the counter were a flower vase with fresh flowers, an electric kettle, two cups and dishes, and also all the ingredients needed to make a cup of tea or coffee, and enjoy it with delicious biscuits. All of this was "on the house". There were even a few books and a writing tablet. Also there was a small television set and a phone. Lya called to ask him if he would like to have his dinner at the inn. Ryan replied: "Yes, I would like to." Lya replied: "Please come downstairs at seven." Ryan was tired. He pulled down the bed and readily fell asleep, listening to the soothing sound of the falling water in the courtyard and the chirping of the birds in the square.

He woke up after a short nap. There was no attached bathroom. He proceeded to the common bathroom for men from the small verandah overlooking the courtyard. At its entrance, there was a place to leave the room-slippers and switch to the bathroom-slippers. Again, he found this to be a strange custom. But he gamely obliged. At about seven in the evening, he went downstairs and was greeted by not Lya but by a middle-aged gentleman, who received him with a smile, and led him to an oblong room with a long wooden table in the middle and a row of wooden chairs on either side of it. Porcelain plates and cutlery were already on the table. Other guests came too, some before and some after Ryan did. When all were seated, the gentleman, who greeted them, introduced himself as Leon. Then he said: "My wife Maya and I run this inn, with the help of our daughter Lya and a few helping hands. When you stay here, you are like a family. So we want you to sit together, get to know each other and enjoy the food." When he had finished, a young boy and a young girl brought a number of dishes of piping hot food in large colorful porcelain bowls. The food was plentiful and delicious. It did not occur to Ryan that there was no meat on the menu, and of course, he did not miss it .The guests were mostly local people, who were traveling within the country. To Ryan's surprise they all spoke to him in English, albeit with a local accent, and were well-aware of what was going on outside their own country. There was also a couple, who like him came from a far-away developed country. But unlike him they were on some business. The local people were very happy to learn that Ryan heard well about their country and came to see it with his own eyes. With no exception they invited him to visit them if he would come to their own town or village. This welcoming gesture to a total stranger was new to him. Ryan heartily accepted their invitation.

After dinner he went out to the square hoping to find some night-life or a bar, of the kinds he had back home and found in many other countries, during his travel. He was disappointed that there was none. But he found a number of eating places, most of which had tables both inside and outside. Here they served not only meals but also drinks and snacks. On each table there was some kind of built-in board game. The customers were mostly local people. They ate and drank happily, conversed rather loudly and laughed heartily. But they did not behave as though they were drunk. And none was obese. He soon found out why. He sat at an outdoor table and ordered a drink and a snack. He noticed that the menu stated in bold letters: We serve only health-giving food and drinks, and in healthy portions. The owner of the restaurant explained that they served wine but only one glass per person. As he tried out different eating places during his stay in the country, he realized that none offered a buffet and there was no "All You Can Eat for $ 3.99" sign. In fact loud bill-boards of all kinds, which ruin townscapes and landscapes elsewhere, were missing here completely. The townscape was dominated by the community buildings in the squares. The only other vertical man-made elements were clusters of wind-turbines tastefully placed away from the settlements, or inside parks and squares.

Ryan knew well that the details of his experiences in Shangri-La would be gradually forgotten by him. Memories did have a way to fade. Yet, his journey was valuable, not only to him but also to many others who had not even heard of Shangri-La, let alone visited the country. So he made it a point to keep meticulous notes of what he saw, what he learnt and how Shangri-La was different from his old world, the one he had left behind at least for now. He also photographed everything that caught his fancy. Thanks to the new modes available, he had no problem in storing almost endless information on very small cameras and recorders. To his pleasant surprise, he also found out that Shangri-La kept up with the times extremely well. Here one could buy or obtain virtually anything one needed. But one could not get weapons, tobacco, hard liquor, drugs and the so-called adult materials. Shangri-La, he realized, was not a back-water country. Instead, it was highly progressive, and seemingly utilized technology judiciously for the well-being of her people.

The next morning, as he came downstairs for breakfast, he saw Lya at the desk in the lobby. He greeted her with folded palms, as the local custom went. "Good morning, Lya," he said, "I did not see you last evening!" Lya replied in her sing-song voice: "I only help out my parents occasionally, mostly with their book-keeping. I spend most of my time working at the Ministry of Well-being. But my hours are fairly flexible." Ryan did not expect to hear this response. He was naturally curious. So he asked her, almost without thinking: "What is this Ministry of Well-Being? And, if you do not mind my asking, what kind of work do you do there?" Lya smiled and replied: "Those are two rather tall questions. Since you wish to know, I shall tell you. But not right now, since it will take some time to explain." Ryan responded: "Fair enough. But, when?" Lya hesitated. Ryan went on: "I go out to the square in the evening after dinner. Will it be too much to ask, if I may have the honor of your company any evening so that you can tell me more." Lya matter-of-factly responded: "Let us do so during a weekday evening." Ryan was elated at the thought. He excused himself and went on with what would become his daily routine.

He wanted to find out for himself if people were indeed mostly in a state of happiness and had a sense of well-being, and if so, then why and how. So he took every opportunity to meet people and visit places. Lya's response saying that she worked at the Ministry of Well-Being made him want to see the place where she worked. He had rented an electric bicycle that provided him with a high degree of mobility. He soon found out that instead of an imposing high-rise building, the Ministry occupied a modest but colorful four-story walk-up building, with elevators for only the elderly, the handicapped and carrying freight.

It was one of several such buildings housing other ministries and various administrative functions of the country. They were placed around a huge landscaped pedestrian plaza with a lake dotted with fountains, in the middle. It was named appropriately, Shangri-La Plaza. Here was a truly people's place. There was abundant provision for walking and sitting, and for festivals, concerts and conventions. It was also simply for enjoying the beauty of nature, whose presence was expressed through the many flowering trees and shrubs, the grassy plains, the mounds, the lake and the many fountains. There were also a number of mobile food stalls. All the buildings had solar panels on their roofs and there were clusters of wind-turbines, between the trees. In front of the buildings there were flags of the country. Ryan parked his electric bicycle in one of the carefully distributed bicycle-parking areas. He mingled with the people who were there not for any business but to enjoy their very own central plaza. It occurred to him that the people-friendly plaza and the placement of the ministerial and administrative buildings around it, visibly symbolized the fact that the functions therein were to serve the people on an equal footing and not to dominate them. There was an unmistakable sense of oneness. It was no wonder that people felt happy here and their faces showed it.

●

Chapter 3. Meeting with Lya: Gross National Well-Being (GNW)

Ryan was eagerly waiting for the day when he would meet Lya again and have the opportunity to talk. It came sooner than he realized. It was a Thursday. Lya had indicated that they could meet in the evening, after dinner, in one of the restaurants on the square in front of their inn. At the appointed hour Ryan went to the restaurant and waited. As befits a lady, Lya showed up a bit later. He greeted her with folded palms as customary and she reciprocated. They sat at an outdoor table at the edge of the sitting area. After a few awkward moments of silence they began to know each other better. Ryan said: "I came from far away to know your famed land, and consider myself truly privileged to meet someone like you, who obviously knows about well-being better than anyone else." Lya blushed and replied: "Thank you for the compliments but I wouldn't say that I'm better than others. I try my best to promote the well-being of our people. The other day you asked me what the Ministry of Well-Being was and what kind of work I did there. I may not be able to answer your questions in one day but let me at least begin." Ryan interrupted: "What would you like to have?" Lya replied: "Just a cup of tea would be fine." Ryan ordered a pot of tea and some small pastries.

Lya continued: "In our way of thinking, people come first and people come last. You may have noticed that my parents and I gave you only our first names. We reject the idea of any middle or last names, which indicate a person's religion, belief etc., or any reference to one's parents' names or even his or her village name. Essentially, in this country people have only one name. However, parents do give their children arbitrary middle and last names, only to keep up with international travel, financial requirements and the like. The reason is pretty simple. In most, if not all countries, a name very often gives away a person's socio-economic standing and he or she is treated accordingly. We do not want that essentially divisive system. In fact, here we deliberately choose names which have an international flavor. The only liberty my parents took in naming me was to take bits of their own names, Leon and Maya, and join them romantically, I would say. Hence, I am Malya or simply Lya. Depending on the country, Malya can mean a garland, a queen or a star of the sea. How about it!" The thought that flashed through Ryan's mind was: "She lives up to all three meanings."

Unaware of what Ryan was thinking about her, Lya continued: "Let's go back to what we were talking about. We measure development and progress in terms of the well-being of all our citizens as individuals and also of the nation as a whole. We measure Gross National Well-Being or GNW, based on frequent formal and informal surveys of the degree of well-being of our people, as opposed to measuring the Gross Domestic Product or GDP. Essentially, to do what needs to be done, to achieve the well-being of our people, we have the Ministry of Well-Being. I work mostly on policy formulation. Since we deal with a good bit of unquantifiable or subjective issues, we constantly modify our methods as per the needs of the people. You may say that we are people-intensive." With a twinkle in her eyes, she asked the almost speechless Ryan: "How was that for starters?"

Ryan responded: "Very impressive. It is so new and yet so appealing as a concept that I am lost for words. But let me try. What do you exactly mean by well-being?" Lya spoke gently: "Essentially well-being expresses itself in terms of happiness. To analyze happiness must be one of the most difficult tasks in the world and yet it does not diminish its validity one bit. The Declaration of Independence of the United States of America lists Life, Liberty and pursuit of Happiness as three inalienable rights of her citizens. There is no happiness unless there is life, which to me equates with health, and there is no happiness unless there is liberty or freedom. Thus foremost of all, we seek happiness for all our people. A rose is beautiful. But when we take out petal after petal what remains? Not a rose but a lifeless nothing. The same applies to happiness, which is most beautiful. But if we attempt to take out the petals of happiness, we may end up with one big nothing. So we simply ask people: "Are you happy?", and almost never: "Why are you happy?" But if need be, happiness can be measured even in numerical terms, using the same method that doctors use to measure pain, or businesses use to measure customer satisfaction, on a scale of 1 to 10. But since we wish our people to be truly happy, we need not quantify happiness on any scale. Have I confused you enough?" Ryan was somewhat dazed but responded: "Not at all. I find what you are saying, fascinating. Please go on."

Lya replied: "If you insist. As I was saying we do not ask people why they are happy. Instead we ask ourselves all the time what makes people happy, and even more than that, what paths we can follow to assure the well-being of our people as directly as possible. No matter how the world changes the basic needs of the people do not change. Human beings still remain about six feet tall and they still need food, clothing and shelter to suit their bodies. Their brains also have hardly changed since they left their homeland in Africa several million years ago. The basic requirement to fulfill their mental needs remain essentially the same. So we start with a human being, keep the human being constantly in our minds, and end with the human being. It is commonly said that nothing is constant but change. But that is an invitation for disaster, since we forget that we are also an integral part of the animal kingdom and nature, and while we can strive to improve the conditions for the fulfillment of our basic needs, our minds and bodies have their human limits. What I am trying to say is that we need not and cannot dance to any and all changes which are thrown at us, without questioning if they are in harmony with our bodies and minds. If we do, we can be torn apart physically and mentally." Ryan was surprised by Lya's way of thinking. It was all new to him. He said: "I see a bit of the point you are making but find it confusing nonetheless."

Lya replied: "I do not blame you one bit. Most people in the world do not think that way. Let me give you some concrete examples of our limits and why we cannot cope with unlimited changes. Take a house, for instance. During the postwar years the size of an average home has grown some two to three hundred percent. But human body size has not, except temporarily in the cases of obesity. Now you can have lots of supersize rooms and fill them up with lots of supersize furniture and gadgets. But are you not diminishing yourself in turn? The very word "cozy" is almost synonymous with comfort and intimacy. How can a house, which overwhelms one by its sheer size, be cozy or intimate? It cannot. But should it not? This change strains one in so many different ways. Physically, mentally, and of course, financially. We probably will discuss the details later. Thus this change, increasing the sizes of homes by two or three hundred percent, cannot and need not be sustained by our minds and bodies and our financial resources." Reflecting on the mega-mansion he had left behind, Ryan nodded in agreement and said: "But what does the size of a house have to do with well-being?" Lya responded: "A lot. That was only an example, albeit a very basic and important one .We try to use the principle of optimum consumption, which fulfills human needs optimally in all aspects of life. A house that fits the needs of our people is easier and less expensive to build, to maintain, to heat and cool, and to clean. It takes up less land, less infrastructure and uses up less resources than a mega-mansion does. In turn, the streets and distances are shorter. One can walk or use a bicycle for most transportation needs. We have more land to spare for nature in the shape of parks and squares, in close proximity to the homes and other buildings. And very importantly, the less land we humans use, the less we have to displace animals from their habitat. After all, they have as much right to live as the human animal. And crucially, their survival is interwoven with ours. So you see Ryan, how mere respecting human scale can have far-reaching consequences." Ryan said: "What you say is so sensible. I wish to know more. Could we continue this very enlightening discussion even as early as tomorrow? At this time would you like to take a walk in this beautiful square? ”

Lya and Ryan bade goodnight to the restaurant people and walked slowly in the square along the carefully laid out and well-lit paths. They were silent at first. Soon Ryan broke the silence: “Pardon my saying so again. I am so privileged to meet you, who seems to know what I think I have been looking for. Shall I have the privilege of seeing you tomorrow again?” Lya hesitated for a moment and responded: “Well, you are such a good listener. I cannot leave you in the middle of my discourse. Yes. We meet but not tomorrow. Shall we say on Saturday, when I do not have to go to the Ministry, and we can meet in the morning, after breakfast? That will also give you a chance to see more of my country in the meantime. How about it?” Ryan replied: “Yes, of course. Let us go back to the inn before your parents begin to worry.” They walked back, bade good night to each other and went to their respective quarters in the inn.

●

Chapter 4. Ryan Ventures Out :: A Typical Family

Next day was a bright sunny one. It felt like spring. Ryan could not quite define why, but he felt good. He wondered about where to go and remembered that many of the guests at his inn had invited him to visit them. So he packed a small bag and set out on his electric bicycle to visit a newly-made friend, who lived in a small town about fifty kilometers away. He had learnt that texting or using a cell-phone while riding any vehicle including bicycles or even while walking, was strictly prohibited, for safety and also for people to be respectful to the environment. The edge of Nondon appeared almost abruptly and the countryside began. Unlike in most towns and cities that he had seen during his world tour, there was no sprawl. There were occasional farmhouse clusters. But, no sprawl. The road was two-lane and lined with flowering shade trees. There were many other cyclists, occasional electric cars and a few electric mini-buses. He waved at fellow cyclists and they waved back with a smile. There were also beautiful places by the road where one could stop, rest and have a picnic. He stopped at one and had a snack. Others did likewise and offered to share their own food with him. He was taken by the warmth of the people to a stranger like him. He also happily reciprocated.

The next town arrived in only an hour. There was a distinct edge to the town. He could see the tight-knit and colorful housing clusters, with their roof-top solar panels and wind turbines and the high roofs of the community buildings, from a distance. With the aid of his GPS he located his friend Sam's house easily. It was around noon. Sam and his wife Tara were expecting him. They exchanged hearty greetings. Here again he exchanged his shoes for the house-sleepers. He was impressed by the beauty of the inside of the house, particularly by its efficient use of space. Not a centimeter was wasted. The living room was small, but well-furnished. It was matted all over. The furnishings were sparse and just in the right places. He was offered a nutritious and tasty lunch by the lady of the house. Again, like at the inn, he did not realize that there was no meat and he did not miss it. After the leisurely lunch, he started to say "goodbye". But the couple would have none of it. They insisted that Ryan spend the night at their place. This kind of ready friendship and hospitality to a virtual stranger, which he was, was new to him.

In the evening over dinner and a glass of wine, he asked Sam: “What is it that makes people here so considerate even to strangers like me? Are you not afraid that he may take advantage of your hospitality?” Sam replied: “We are taught from early childhood to value well-being above all. There are many aspects of well-being. Some can be measured in terms of numbers like the level of education, some in terms of comparison of factors like comfort and convenience, and some which cannot be measured like “a million dollar smile” or love, but when all or most go well, we are happy. There are many ways to find happiness. Making others happy is certainly one of them. We are happy if you are happy to be with us. Of course we can tell with a good bit of certainty if a stranger is not to be trusted. That is no exact science. Trust, first of all, is a mutual thing. When a stranger like you accepts our friendship and hospitality, he shows that he trusts us too. Further, it is our custom to treat a guest like a part of the family and possibly he feels it. We know down deep in our hearts that he values that in his heart too. Am I right?” Ryan agreed. He reflected on similar experiences back home and knew that Sam was right. He slept in the living room itself, after a hidden bed was pulled down from the wall. Lying in it he thought of the days he had spent in Shangri-La. He thought of Lya's beautiful face. Here was a person who was so intelligent and informed, and yet so gentle. He wondered if she felt the same way as he felt toward her. He could not decide. Women were so inscrutable, he thought. Oh, well. There was precious little he could do about it. Gradually he fell asleep.

He was aroused by the bleating of some farm animals. This, he was not used to. Tara explained to him: "We all maintain a small garden in the rear and raise a few sheep or goats for milk. That helps us with some ready fresh food. But not all. We do have markets, where one can buy fresh vegetables, fruits, nuts, whole-grain rice, whole-wheat bread, pulses and many other health-giving foods. We virtually use no processed foods and find no need for them. Health is extremely important to us. What is life, if there is no health?" Ryan asked: "But doesn't processed food save one from the drudgery of spending a lot of time on cooking?" Tara responded: "Indeed it may. However, we find pleasure in preparing food and eating it in the right atmosphere, preferably with other members of the family and friends like you. In effect we take nourishing the body, as one of the most important activities of life. What is the point in saving time from something that is vitally important? Saving time for what? After all, we save time to do something that makes us happy. Our prime goal is the well-being of individuals and not merely increasing gross domestic product. We find it rather difficult to understand, the idea of having a "business lunch", at which club sandwiches are passed around and gulped down with coffee. The joy of eating is sacrificed to business. The health implications of the process are enormous. My friend, it is not for us." Ryan had not thought of it that way. But still he rebelled and thought that the ritual of cooking and eating over a long period was too slow and too wasteful for precious time. Since in his own country, as in many other developed countries, both husband and wife worked, that too often fulltime, how could they possibly find time to cook? And how could they make both ends meet if both husband and wife did not work? Perhaps the answer lay in optimum consumption as Lya had explained. He decided that he had to think about it more. He got a clearer answer much later from Lya: "Everyone worked, consumption was optimum, maximizing income was not a priority, and health and hence social life were of paramount interest. So no one worked like a workaholic."

Sam asked Ryan if he would like to visit the nearby square with him. Ryan eagerly agreed. He observed that in one tree-covered corner of the square, there was a good-size brick-paved area with a few small shelters. There were benches and low tables on the sides, for sitting and reading newspaper or whatever, or just people-watching. Here many people were doing various exercises, some freehand and some with simple equipment. Quite a few were jogging, going around the inside of the entire square, and others were enjoying a walk. Ryan asked his friend if he would like to join the activities. He smiled and replied: "Not today. I want to give you glimpses into our day-to-day lives. As you visit more friends you will get a more complete picture. I hope you like what you see and also tell us how you think we can do better."

Ryan asked: "Do you have indoor facilities like we have, and we call them gymnasiums, swimming pools and indoor arenas etc., which are open even in the evenings and throughout the year? Suppose I don't have time during the day and want to exercise, swim or play some indoor games in the evening." Sam answered: "We do have such facilities but not too many, since they cut us off from nature, promote the rather unnatural habit of treating the night as a day, and of being insensitive to the beauty of full or partial darkness. Also importantly it is very wasteful in terms of energy-usage. Not so long ago, when energy was not so plentiful, outdoor playfields, arenas and the like served us well, and they do so even now. When we have indoor facilities like the community buildings, they serve many purposes. But they are not commonplace." Given his own background, Ryan could not readily agree with Sam's argument. He did agree that the tendency to treat night as day, and carry out any and all activities at night, having day-light effect in too many places, took a toll on human minds and physique. But being used to night-life back home from his early childhood, he was not sure if largely doing away with it would be workable, or even acceptable to most countries. Yet he also liked the concept of viewing night and day altogether differently, as rather natural.

Ryan felt a special urge to return to Nondon and see Lya again. Being away from her even for two days made him impatient. After lunch at Sam and Tara's place, he profusely thanked them and said "good-bye". They made him promise to visit them again before long. Tara had a packet of food ready for his trip back .A thoroughly overwhelmed Ryan set out for Shangri-La. He really felt that he was leaving a part of his family behind. A strangely new feeling it was.

●

Chapter 5. In Nature :: Life Above All

Ryan had called Lya earlier. As per their plan they met after breakfast. Thereupon they made a trip to a market, bought some food and rode their electric bicycles to a national park, that was located only ten kilometers away from Nondon. The place was Lya's choice. She came here often to be with nature and to recharge her inner self. She wanted to talk in depth to a curious Ryan about the thinking and approach of Shangri-La. And she hoped that when he returned to his homeland, he would spread the word about what Shangri-La really stood for; that it was not a mere wishful dream but a country which embodied much of what made good sense, to not only the people of her own country but many thinkers world over. Unfortunately, such sense was often being ignored elsewhere for the sake of maximizing GDP, instead of widespread well-being. It was not easy to explain but one had to try, particularly to one like Ryan who really wanted to know. They soon arrived at the park entrance. There was no ticket gate and hence no tickets to purchase. There was a visitors' center well inside the park. It was attended by two young ladies. At the heart of the park was a lake, with a pedestrian-cum-bicycle path encircling it and a number of campsites with picnic grounds dotting its shore. Lya and Ryan found a quiet place near the lake and settled down. Lya prepared some tea using a grill provided by the park.

She said: "If you are wondering why I have selected the park, it is because we can talk here as undisturbed as one can be. I really want to tell you some things about the essence of our country's approach to development. It is not a complete story since we are dealing with many things which are not easily measurable. Please feel free to interrupt me at any time. We start with Life, it being the most precious thing not only to us, you and me as individuals, but to all in this world, including all animals and plants. Life is the most precious thing in the entire Universe, for there is no proof yet that it exists anywhere else, no proof yet even though a growing number of scientists believe that the endless Universe is teeming with Life. Interestingly, recently astronomers have detected two enormous planets many light-years away, which are made entirely of diamond. Imagine what would happen to the value of diamond on Earth if a diamond asteroid would pass by the Earth and our great scientists and engineers would find a way to mine it. Can you imagine that the value of Life being diminished, even if there is Life elsewhere!" Ryan asked: "Why are you saying this? Don't we all value Life most of all?"

Lya replied: "Perhaps, but do you see it mentioned ever in anyone's policy or development plan except in the Declaration of Independence of the United States? Ironically, people all over the world take Life so much for granted that they wake up to its literally unspeakable value only when they are about to lose their own or that of someone very dear to them. In their misguided rush for material wealth and earthly gratifications they become oblivious to the greatest treasure of them all. Everything else but Life appears on their mind's screen. It is one of the saddest things in the world that they do not think of Life at all when they have it. It is not just individuals, even countries do likewise."

Ryan was taken aback by the intensity of Lya's voice. He said: "But Life cannot be defined as easily as material objects. Everyone values love and affection too and very much so." Lya replied almost impatiently: "Life can indeed be defined very easily. It is expressed through the health of our minds and bodies. As long as we remain healthy we are alive. It is true that Life ends inevitably, no matter how healthy we remain till the end. Unfortunately people all over the world are taught at every step of their education to compete. Compete for what? To possess and consume more and more of material objects and outdo others in this mad rush? We can live under the grand illusion that we possess more power or glory if we "win". We seldom stop to think of the consequences. No, my dear Ryan, that cannot be the path to go, for it has no end, and most importantly, it contributes nothing to the most valuable treasure we have, Life." Ryan stopped listening to anything beyond those words "my dear Ryan". Looking at Ryan's face Lya suddenly realized that her words might have touched him in an unintentional way. She immediately changed the topic and proposed that they take a walk along the shore of the lake. She had a lot more to say but felt that a pause was called for.

They walked silently. Ryan reflected on what Lya was saying including the words of endearment. But he realized that it was just a figure of speech. Or was that all? Lya felt a bit embarrassed. She herself wondered if her words betrayed her feelings for this stranger. She was not sure. Neither she nor Ryan paid much attention to it, at least for now. As they walked their conversation resumed. Ryan asked: “I agree that Life is most precious but what does it have to do with economic development? Is it not the backbone of well-being?” Lya replied: “On the surface, yes. But, by itself, no. When the emphasis of life changes from material possession to Life itself, people turn inwards. They realize that there is no point in accumulating and consuming more and more material goods, in competing for material possessions, and in exerting power over others; and that the first and foremost task is to seek health of their own bodies and minds. Ironically health comes from optimum consumption of food and energy, zero consumption of harmful things like tobacco, sugar, saturated fats and hard liquor, and optimum exercise of both mind and body. Maximizing consumption and so-called power can only do harm to one’s health, meaning Life and that too only at a tremendous and unsustainable financial cost.” Ryan interrupted: “How’s that? I am lost. I always thought that consumption is what keeps the wheels of economy turning.”

Lya replied: "That's why I said earlier "on the surface, yes". If maximizing consumption is one's prime goal, where do you draw the line? What will happen when the Earth's resources are exhausted, as they inevitably will be? What happens when the Earth's air and water are all polluted because of burning fossil fuels and coal, as if there is no end to them, and indiscriminate waste disposal? What happens when the world's forest cover dwindles as it is doing very rapidly, due to sprawl among other things, and animal species become extinct under our very own eyes? Who will pollinate the flowers if bee population is decimated as it is happening right now? I can go on, since the list of damage caused by humans in a mere century is a long one. Even though leaders of many countries are beginning to see what is happening, few have the political or moral courage to ask their own people, or even ask themselves, to rein in consumption. Instead, the countries are competing with each other for the rapidly exhausting resources. Worse still, they are knowingly using the labors of the poorer countries for their own gains in spite of the laborers often living in dire conditions, and worse still, as slaves. Whereas apparent economic gains, measured as GDP, often paint a pretty picture, such gains are increasingly limited to those who already have plenty, at the cost of the vast majority of have-nots."

Ryan interrupted Lya at this point: "Isn't it true that the rate of poverty is falling in many countries whose GDPs are rising?" Lya replied: "If one goes by published statistics about poverty figures by themselves that is perhaps true. But the percentages hardly depict the real story. The sheer number of people who remain poor or go hungry or suffer from malnutrition generation after generation is staggering. Today the poor numbers 1.7 billion or one quarter of the world's population. The number of hungry or malnourished is 1.02 billion or one in seven of world's population. Even more sadly, one in three of these are children. Is it any comfort to these hapless billions, oh yes, billions, that increasing GDP is reducing their overall percentage but not their absolute numbers? Is there a global scarcity of food? Not really. A staggering one-third of all food produced in the world goes waste. Can they find solace in the uncertain fact that some decades later their children or grandchildren may, just may, fare better, that too if all the road blocks are removed ? For that there is absolutely no certainty. How do they feel when from their miserable existence they can look at the almost sinfully lavish lifestyles of some of their fellow human beings? Also at what cost is GDP rising? Are we going to deliver a barren earth to our future generations? Must we? No, we must not and do not need to. This is why I am trying to focus on what is most valuable in life." Ryan merely said: "I am beginning to see where you are taking me. But can we take a break first? Can we briefly switch to such a mundane subject as lunch?" Lya was amused by this sudden turn in the discussion. She looked at Ryan's sad face and readily agreed that they must stop and have lunch.

Lya pulled out a number of surprises. She had already figured out what Ryan liked to eat and took care to buy at the market some of the foodstuff which came close to non-vegetarian foods in taste and appearance. These included whole-wheat products, tofu, mushroom, pulse-products and cottage cheese. Along with multiple spices, these are used extensively by vegetarians to prepare highly tasty and health-giving meals. Additionally she had bought fresh fruits and greens. Deftly, she prepared meals for themselves using a few utensils on the grill. Ryan tried to assist her. She had allowed him to make the fire, but all in all, she found him to be clumsy and absolutely useless. Consequently, she bade him to spend the time enjoying the beauty of nature or writing his diary. He somewhat grudgingly complied with her wishes while stealing frequent and admiring glances at her reddened face and elegant movements. The lunch was ready and Lya said: "You can help now by setting up the table." Ryan was happy to be useful. He admitted that even a meat-and-potatoes man like him enjoyed the food very much, prepared as it was by such a special person. He said: "You are a cook par excellence." Lya was embarrassed, but merely said: "It's nothing. You are being too generous."

Ryan knew that the entire country had adopted vegetarianism. He also knew some of the benefits but wanted to know more. He asked: "Why do you have only vegetarian food?" Lya responded: "There are so many reasons that I don't know where to start. There is a taboo about talking anything negative about eating flesh. So please take what I am going to say in stride. We feel that the civilized species of humans, unlike some other animals, could rise above killing other animals, to satisfy hunger. No matter how humanely an animal is killed, it is still killing. It is doubtful if a child could actually see how and where-from meat comes, he or she would like to consume it. Have you noticed the joy a child has in a petting zoo! We find it hard to understand why hunting is called a sport, even though in almost all cases it involves finding joy in inflicting utter pain to a hapless and often gorgeously beautiful animal, which does not stand a chance against a high-powered rifle. Where is chivalry in that? Where is fairness in that? Even animals do not kill for fun. If we are "pro-life" as we should be, and fight for not destroying an embryo, how can we justify killing animals? Some may justify killing animals in the name of "culling", to bring a balance in the animal population versus their food supply or available habitat. Why not let nature do it? And why not give them more room and connecting corridors for migration instead? It is one of the greatest ironies that we are trying so hard to find life elsewhere in space or in our very own solar system and casually destroying the same here, even when they are posing no threat to us and when instead they enliven nature. Anyway, I must tell you that we do not oblige anyone to be a vegetarian, but neither do we condone eating meat. No one will tell you not to eat it but people will tell you why one should not. It simply does not suit our policy of optimum consumption or our policy of being in harmony with nature."

Lya continued: "Based on the best information we have, a very size-able share of all grains produced in the world goes toward feeding animals. Just imagine how many hungry mouths could be fed instead. We can add to that, the very serious health and environmental costs as well as the much greater land requirements to raise animals. It is also not true that humans must consume animal protein to remain healthy. Combinations of vegetable proteins can provide excellent substitutes and perhaps instinctively people all over the world have been consuming exactly that since millenniums. The question comes up: What about consuming fish and other creatures of the sea, the lake and the river? Ironically, many of the objections which are true for eating land-based animals do not hold good for water-based animals. In fact most of them contribute to good health by way of providing flesh which is free from saturated fat and oil which is rich in highly beneficial omega-3 fatty acids. But the cruel aspect of killing an animal to satisfy our hunger remains. We do not prevent anyone from eating fish either: however most of Shangri-Lans, including of course me, choose not to. But in all circumstances we make sure that any animal consumed is killed in the least painful method possible. It is not the ideal solution but it is the best we can do, without encroaching upon people's freedom. We value freedom very highly in all spheres of life, but we also draw a line when one's freedom threatens another's. I am sure we will talk about it at length in the future."

After lunch, Ryan took the lead: "I often wonder if all the countries would decide one fine day that they have little to gain by waging wars, occupying others' land, acquiring their resources and worse still, enslaving their people. Yet since the end of World War II, there have been the so-called Cold War and also a number of regional hot wars. Now there is a new kind of war, which has no fronts and no boundaries. And the weapons today are not only the huge and visible ones but also the invisible ones. Enormous amounts of global resources are spent in offense and defense. The actual figures are staggering: $ 1.6 trillion in 2010 or 2.6 % of global GDP, but as high as 20% of the national budget and an incredible

30% of the national tax revenues of some countries! Add to that the cost of loss of life and unspeakable suffering of millions, and the adverse impact of literally wiped out villages, towns and even cities. Also add to that the huge cost of rehabilitation and rebuilding. Even a fraction of all that, if spent for well-being purposes, could most likely wipe out all or most of the miseries in those countries and the entire world . But the big question remains: how does one make it happen? How to cut back on the cost of raising and maintaining massive armed forces and divert the funds to constructive purposes?"

Ryan never spoke like this before. Lya almost could not believe her ears. She said very gently: "My dear Ryan, you are thinking about the same problem that must be occupying many eminent minds. There is no easy answer but here we try to go to the root of the problem. I am sorry to bring back the issue of 'Life' as the most valuable possession that one can have. Once we understand this deeply in our hearts we do not crave for "possessions", for we know that except for the essential means for living, by way of optimum food, clothing and shelter, merely possessing more adds nothing to the joy of living. We only need to strive to enjoy 'Life' and that we can do by staying well in body and mind. This is easier said than done. Because , most unfortunately there is a very widespread tendency to view enjoying 'Life' in terms of eating, drinking and being merry, that too better or more than others, or worse still, by depriving the vast majority of people and even enslaving fellow human beings, and with no concern about the fate of our environment. Herein comes our new approach."

"Here I go," said Lya. "This is extremely important. We teach our children to look at the entire world as their own family. We teach them that we are riding a spaceship called The Earth. Today's children understand that concept very easily, since they are born in the age of moon-landing, space stations, satellites carrying robots to Mars, Hubble Telescope photographing galaxies at the edge of the Universe and so much more. Our children are born global citizens. They can easily be made to understand that they are part of a global family, which is riding the spaceship, Earth. They will easily understand that if the spaceship has finite supplies then we have to use them most judiciously. They will know that if we wish to breathe the air on the spaceship and drink the water, we have to keep them clean. You see Ryan, how simple it is!" Ryan merely said: "Yes. I can hardly wait to hear more." Lya enthusiastically continued: "Instead of starting with the concept of the nuclear family, we start from the opposite end. We teach them that nations are mere subdivisions of the global family, and step by step, we come to a community, a joint family, a nuclear family and finally, only finally, the individual. This awareness of the individual being an integral part of the global family is the foundation of our social order. This is virtually the opposite of what is taught conventionally. Unlike in other lands, where the nuclear family and its interests come first and people feel lost when that unit breaks up, as it does all too often, individuals living in a global family are never alone. And shall I say that they have little incentive to be selfish. If we think hard, it is selfishness that spoils all the good intentions behind all good plans, policies and isms". Ryan agreed for he had seen this back home too. He wondered how selfishness, which leads to greed, corruption, nepotism and gross indifference toward the suffering of fellow human beings, can be removed and began to realize that what Lya was saying so patiently was like a breath of fresh air.

Lya knew that Ryan understood. She added: "I have compared the Earth to a spaceship, but I need to add that there is a major difference. The spaceships our children already know about are all man-made. Even though "HAL", the live computer in "2001 Space Odyssey", was alive, the rest of the ship was not. The Earth is not man-made and she is alive in her entirety. Starting from the inner molten core to the outer crust and the air-mass above, she is in constant motion and in a state of constant renewal. We call her Mother Earth, since she, along with the Sun, provides us with all the nourishment that we need. We also call her Mother Nature. We teach our children these concepts and they are very receptive or shall I say, understanding? They know that it is imperative that we take care of her as she takes care of us all, and that we take from her only what we need for our well-being and no more, and very importantly, we help her sustain the ability to offer us the bounty without any end. There are natural resources which are finite. As it is, it is already difficult to extract them and the human and environmental costs in doing so are enormous. We cannot cut down our forests without turning the land into deserts and dust-bowls, and destroying animal habitats. We cannot pollute our rivers, seas and oceans and create dead-zones, which support no life. Our children understand that even though there are natural cycles of global warming and cooling, a la mini ice ages, which are beyond our control, we can and should prevent or minimize the pollution of our atmosphere, or risk endangering our health and the health of our most benevolent friend, the plant world. Given this kind of understanding, we teach our children the value in striving for the betterment of the global community instead of amassing of possessions for their own gratification, the value in helping nature to sustain herself instead of exploiting her to the breaking point, the value in protecting the flora and fauna, the value in being healthy in mind and body and in valuing 'Life' above all."

She added: "You have been an excellent listener, Ryan. We deserve to have a break from my monologues. How about some tea and then a walk, before we head for home? " Ryan was thinking the same. He was touched by her sensitivity toward his needs. He happily agreed and said: "Your so-called monologues are so enlightening that I want to have more of them. I can tell that you have a lot more to say and have just begun. When shall we continue again?" Lya replied: "Thank you for the compliments, Ryan. Indeed there is a lot more and it will be my pleasure to share them with you. Shall we try in the middle of the week, say Wednesday in the evening, after my work? Perhaps in the mean time you would like to visit a school to find out how we "catch them young" and mold them to be good global citizens. I shall inform a nearby school in advance, so that someone will receive you and show you around."

●

Chapter 6. To a School :: Catch Them Young

Ryan thought about how intensely Lya had talked about teaching the children ways to be good global citizens and he was eager to see it firsthand. After breakfast one day, he walked to the designated school, which like most facilities in the area, was not too far away. This was because the entire capital was planned as a compact and space-efficient city with well-defined edges and because there was neither sprawl nor very wide roads. The school consisted of a cluster of large pavilions of varied sizes with interconnecting covered passages and a series of landscaped courtyards in-between. There was a large garden with fruit trees in front, a large playground in the rear and vegetable gardens on the two sides. Since teachers and students alike walked to the school there was no need for a parking lot. By now Ryan had learnt to remove his shoes and switch to the school-slippers. He was greeted by an amiable man in his forties. He introduced himself as Chandra. As was customary, they had some tea first. Ryan said: "I have heard so much about your education system that I truly wish to know much more. Please tell me how your system differs from conventional systems elsewhere."

Chandra replied: "Please allow me to tell you first that I am known as the "First Teacher", since teaching is our prime task. Elsewhere I would be known as the "Principal" or the "Headmaster". When it comes to a university, we use the "First Professor" instead of the "President" or the "Vice Chancellor". In Shangri-La we try to avoid titles that create divisions. Anyway, I'd like to tell you that our system is highly flexible, since it is not conventional, and we are always responding to the needs as we perceive them or identify them. We do not have a graded program and the best thing is that no one fails. As such, no one is penalized for failing. Every student is motivated to do his or her best, set their own pace of development and except for certain basic knowledge of the conventional subjects like "reading, writing and arithmetic" and "history and geography", they are free to, and in fact encouraged to, follow areas of their greatest interests and proficiency. They are not taught to compete, with one exception, which is to improve one's own self as a human being. I know that it is extremely difficult to improve one's own self, but essentially it means being healthy in body and mind, thinking of the entire human family, rather than the narrow confines of a nuclear family, and of the entire ecosystem. All this may sound grandiose but we believe that such thoughts can be and must be taught from day one, for it is much easier to do that than when their minds are already narrowed down. Children are very open and they are prone to love "thy neighbor as thyself" so easily." Ryan was impressed with what he had heard thus far. He merely asked: "Please tell me in concrete terms how you achieve your noble goals."

Chandra replied: "They sound lofty but really we view the entire socio-physical fabric of the environment, in which the children grow up, as a very large classroom in which and from which they learn. They take cues from the grown-ups and the environment they live in. We teach them by being exemplary ourselves, and we studiously shun anything which would create a double standard, one for them and one for the adults. As you probably have already found out, we do not have anything like a nightlife, which includes bars or taverns, so-called adult-entertainment and gambling casinos, for we do not believe that we can justify any of those to our children with a straight face, and tell them that it is alright for us but not for them. Whereas we do not ban some video games for group playing, we reject the idea that gory and violent games are okay, for it does not take a nuclear physicist or extensive research to determine their harmful effect on one's mind. Instead of preventing them from watching those, we create an environment both at home and at school, so that they play outdoors and have little incentive to play video games. Ah yes. We even let our children have a few drops of wine on special occasions. In this context I'd like to add that we do not subscribe to the idea of "us" and "them" in any sphere of life, since we see nothing but confusion result from it. We however have great cultural programs and festivals, both indoor and outdoor, in which a whole family and even a whole community can participate. We do use projections on large screens extensively for classroom use as well as community learning or entertainment, and discourage the students from sitting alone at a computer or using their miscellaneous media gadgets mindlessly. I am reminded of the great architect Frank Lloyd Wright's calling television as the "chewing gum for the eyes".

Chandra continued: "I'm sorry that I got a bit carried away. I think you meant to ask me how we impart knowledge and wisdom in a classroom setting. We also divide our schools into elementary, middle and high schools like in conventional systems, so that out-of-country transfers are easy. We do maintain some separation between the three but also allow them to come together for outdoor programs like gardening and sports, in which the big brothers and sisters can guide the little ones. Another time when they can share is during lunch. I forgot to mention that the children bring their own lunch from their homes; thus they get a good home-cooked meal, which they often share with their friends. We do encourage sharing and also the big boys and girls mentoring the little ones, so the older ones set good examples and the little ones behave. We, the teachers, act as the biggest brothers and sisters. This is not too unlike the system followed by the "Scouts". We carry this spirit inside the classrooms too, where various subjects are taught. Instead of teaching subjects as separate entities we strive to link them up with lessons of life. For example, since we put a lot of emphasis on health, we teach the children how food started to be cultivated at different times, in different countries, using what tools, at what cost, their nutritious values or lack of it, how diseases occur, how to prevent them from occurring in the first place, how and why famines take place, what role climate plays in food production and so on. We tell them to write down what they have learnt, and read their writings out loud for all to hear. We tell them to research using various sources, like books, visits and interviews, and how to bring about improvements where something is lacking. You will agree, that it is a dynamic process, which invites self-reliance, teamwork and innovation on the part of both teachers and students." Ryan asked: "But how do you ensure that the students have learnt what they are expected to learn through a conventional curriculum?" Chandra replied: "We are constantly evaluating their progress and I am happy to tell you that we find that our students learn not only what is covered by the conventional curriculums but also far beyond them; we conduct tests throughout the time they spend here, but there are no annual examinations. We are happy that they are prepared well to live, for they find no disconnect between what they learn at school and the world outside."

Ryan asked: "What do you do with what the children produce in the vegetable gardens?" Chandra replied: "I am glad that you asked. We take food very seriously since it provides us sustenance. We also place a lot of value on the process of cooking, in which our children participate at home, and eating, which when done together as a family and with respect, binds the family together. Through the production of food, our children connect with Mother Earth very directly, and develop an understanding of the importance of ecology, how to sustain the fertility of soil, and how to use rain water collected from the roofs and through other means. In our gardens we also maintain some livestock, like goats and sheep. The children tend to all of them. Now, what do we do with the food? We simply distribute it among the families of the students and the teachers. The entire process is managed by the students themselves, with some help from the teachers as needed. As you will agree they learn a lot of management, mathematics and other areas through the entire process. Above all they get a lot of good exercise, fresh air and sun. Naturally they love it."

Ryan asked: "Do you have competitive sports? I mean do they prepare to compete with other schools or let's say other countries?" Chandra replied: "They play lots of games but we take special care to build up team spirit, and the composition of the teams is rotated constantly. We have no cheer-leaders and we do not allow parents to cheer from the sidelines. The emphasis is on participation and not merely winning. Yes, they play with other schools but the end goal is not winning or losing, which carried to the extreme, can lead to violence even. We often mix up teams from various schools and have much more fun this way than if they were strictly defined by respective schools. This process of give-and-take makes our children, our future citizens, more understanding and compassionate toward fellow citizens. After all, our aim is to prepare them to be good global citizens."

Chandra continued: "Very importantly, we wish to have one hundred percent literacy, meaning much more than mere ability to read and write. Among other things, we feel that democracy to work well requires well-informed and wise citizens. You may be wondering why I am adding the word "wise". It is because mere information or knowledge does not automatically impart understanding or wisdom. For that one needs to be informed but one also needs to analyze, synthesize and contemplate on the information in one's own mind. Some of today's gadgets and "search-engines" provide tons and tons of information. People using them feel they are gaining wisdom. There is a danger in that. First of all they do not become wise and secondly they famously ignore wisdom which comes with contemplation, age and experience. I say: Enough of that. How about some lunch? No, no, you need not bring your own. I have already informed all our teachers. You will share with us and also get to know them."

Ryan readily accepted the invitation. There was a good bit of exchange of food and he sampled as much as he could. Once again, all the foods were vegetarian and lean, but they satisfied his meat-and-potatoes taste buds. Over tea he asked: "How do you rejuvenate your knowledge and understanding and keep up to date with the world?" One teacher answered: "Virtually all of us also work in the outside world with institutions or organizations of our choice such as, universities, research institutions, various industries and National or Regional Service agencies. It is a two-way give-and-take proposition; we stay up to date and we also constantly innovate ways for betterment."

Another teacher added: "There are many areas of technological development which concern us for their impact on our children. So we research how best we can utilize them instead of their taking the upper hand. For example, television, which is a wonderful gadget if viewed judiciously but a highly negative influence if viewed indiscriminately and for too long. So we try to find ways to limit viewing only to good programs and for limited hours. We have decided that not every child needs to have a set in his or her own room. This fits well with our national policy to have optimum consumption and also developing strong family bond. Thus we do not have the so-called "couch-potatoes" and obesity. One may pooh-pooh such research as mundane but we do not. What would be the point of researching if our research cannot help put our house in order first and foremost!" Ryan was overwhelmed by the thoughtfulness of the teachers. It all made a lot of sense. He liked the flexibility of the system and the whole concept of knitting it all together. He thanked Chandra and all the teachers for the insight they provided and the delicious lunch and bade them "good-bye". Chandra said: "It was a great pleasure having you with us. We hope that you will visit us again."

●

Chapter 7. Getting to Know Lya :: Social Customs

Wednesday evening finally arrived. Ryan was missing not seeing Lya during what seemed to be an interminably long time. He admired her greatly, for her wisdom and for her devoting so much of her personal time to a stranger like him. To her, he must have looked like a completely naïve person, who knew little about the real world, and had to be taught about everything that was virtually second nature to Lya. Yet there was a subtle joy in virtually submitting to this highly accomplished yet very gentle woman. He had never felt like this about any other woman before. He himself was proud, highly educated, well-to-do and in good health. Lya was all that except that she was not a proud person. She was very gentle. Suddenly, Ryan realized that her gentleness gave her all the strength in the world. He was not ashamed of submitting to this uncommon person.

They met in another square this time, away from Inn Jasmine. These squares were not literally squares in shape, as in the absence of many cars and much automobile traffic there was no great need to have a grid pattern of streets. Also Nondon had grown organically. The streets were narrow with surprises, like small and large squares, always waiting around the corners. Small shops, including restaurants, often of the Mom-and-Pop kind, strung themselves around. There were trees, wind turbines, seating, jogging trails, play areas and fountains in almost all the squares. Some had large community buildings. Lya and Ryan sat at a table in a restaurant and ordered coffee and some lean pastries. Lya: "How was your visit to the school?" Ryan: "As always, beyond expectations. I find the single-mindedness of people here most admirable. It is as if everyone knows what he or she is trying to do and looking for ways to constantly improve upon that. Such sense of purpose is uncommon elsewhere, I believe." Lya admitted that she did not know too much about other countries except that she knew that in democracies the process of finding consensus of opinions, and agreeing on goals and ways to attain them, are all too often clouded by partisanship, due to people's putting much too much emphasis on economic development, competitive advantages and perceived self-interest.

She added: "Here we try our best to keep our focus on common good starting with the well-being of Mother Earth, and then our fellow human beings, and the notion that we must use what she has given us and what we produce eco-sensitively. Toward this, we attempt to use technology to serve us instead of our serving technology. Why I mention this is because of the first reaction of some people to our approach is that we are turning the clock backwards. No, we are not. To the contrary. By avoiding excesses in everything we do, we hope to steadily move forward to our goal of living Life well as long as we live. Please tell me, now that you have seen a school, would you like to know about our higher education system?" Even though Ryan did, he was at the same time wishing to know more about something more personal. He wanted to know more about Lya herself. He answered: "Forgive me, Lya. We have known each other for some time and you have been kind enough to tell me a lot about Shangri-La. I am so grateful for that. Yes I do want to know about the system of higher education. But I know so little about a very special person who has become, for all practical purposes, Shangri-La herself to me. That person is of course you, Lya."

Lya blushed. She also has been sensing that Ryan was beginning to feel close to her. She simply said: "I am a very insignificant person, Ryan. You would be merely wasting your very precious time in learning about me. But if you really want, I shall try. What is it that you want to know?" Ryan replied: "That itself is a difficult question. Just tell me whatever comes to your mind, starting with your childhood." Lya: "You are being wicked. How can a person answer when there is no question? Really! Anyway, let me try. I was born in a hillside village around two hundred kilometers from Nondon. My parents were farmers. I am their only child, even though, the national trend is to have two children per family and we value a girl child no less than a boy child. We understand that unless women are on an equal footing with the men, our country could not progress well. However we do not subscribe to the theory that men and women are the same. Equal, yes, but not the same. We find anything "unisex" a bit strange. Women in our society are regarded in some ways as more than men since they are like Mother Earth. I cannot fully explain this feeling to you. You just have to feel it. You know Ryan, most men do not realize that it is women who gave birth to civilization itself by settling down and raising crops and hard grains, hence surplus food, instead of pursuing animal herds for food and leading a nomadic life. How about that?"

Lya continued: "Now let's go back to my parents and little me. As they became relatively old and had enough savings they sold their farm to a few young people in the village and moved to Nondon. Even though I grew up in a village, my parents made sure that I got a good education. I used to ride an electric-bicycle to the nearby town to attend high school and then college. So did all my friends. After we moved to Nondon, I went to a university and did my Ph.D. in Well-Being." Ryan interjected: "Ph.D. in Well-Being! What a great idea! Where I come from, specialization is the name of the game. Everyone is so focused on a fraction that few understand the totality. When I was a young boy, I could go to the doctor, who could tell in a few minutes what was wrong with me and get me completely cured soon enough. Nowadays more often than not, the general practitioner makes you go through lots of tests, then sends you to "specialists", who in turn focus on their own areas of specialty and leave you cured only so far as their own domains are concerned.

I assume that's because they are unfortunately too hard-pressed for time to look beyond their areas of specialization." Lya listened but did not comment on what Ryan said. She merely said: "I am really a generalist of a generalist."

Ryan asked: "But you have left out so much of what happened before you moved to Nondon. How was your childhood? What did you do other than study?" Lya: "My neighborhood friends and I played simple games like hop-scotch and musical chairs, hide-and-seek using the entire neighborhood as our play-area, had children's picnics in the woods by the river, collected and ate fruits freely from the many orchards, and sometimes just wandered far and wide. As we grew up, we also played soccer, badminton, volleyball and when the weather was bad, board-games. Occasionally we studied too, but playing with friends was so absorbing and fun that I honestly don't remember when I studied at home. We did watch television occasionally, but only occasionally. One thing I must tell you. We did not have much homework, if any, till I went to high school or college. There were no earth-shaking events. Just happy childhood and adolescent years. That's all. Happy?"

Ryan was curious about something else: "Did you date boys when you became a teenager?" Lya laughed heartily and said: "You are being very naughty. Yes, I dated lots of boys but not in the sense that dating means in some other countries. I grew up with many boys and girls, and we would participate in feasts, festivals, dances and the like. But we would not develop any one-to-one special relationship without the knowledge and consent of our parents. You see Ryan, unlike in many other countries, we like to believe that relationships ought to be taken very seriously and that they should have the blessings of the parents, if not of the entire community, for nurturing and sustenance. After all, our parents know us better than anyone else does and they can be objective. Marriage is not just between two individuals. It is in many ways a union between two families. And when there are children as a result of a marriage, they are most deeply involved. Their entire lives depend heavily on the closeness of the relationship between their parents. Marriage is meant to be for life, as the vows tell. For all these reasons we do not think much of what is known as "turn-style marriage". Neither do we have much faith in "no-fault" divorce. As I have mentioned earlier we do all we can to assure the success of a marriage in the first place. Our marriages are meant to last and happily, they do. I have already spoken too much .What else would you like to know?"

Ryan felt a bit embarrassed. He replied: "I should not have asked you that silly question. In your natural wisdom you have not asked me anything about myself but I just have to tell you something very painful, yet very important. This may be as good a time as any to tell you. Lya, I have gone through a no-fault divorce, but most amicably. I just could not help it. Our ways parted beyond any hope. It was the way that I believed in, that led me to Shangri-La." Lya replied: "Ryan, I respect you for telling me what you have just told me. I know in my heart that you would not go through that painful experience if you could have helped it. You were not born and brought up here. I feel that it would not have happened if you were." She did not want to dwell over Ryan's painful experience and proceeded with changing the topic. She asked: "Now that you have visited a school, would you care to visit a university? I shall be most happy to arrange a visit, if you like." Ryan eagerly agreed. In his heart, he admired Lya for her understanding attitude, in the face of her own belief, and what he had just told her. They rode back to the inn without saying many words and bade each other goodnight.

Chapter 8. To a University & Health

Next morning, Ryan rode his electric bicycle to Nondon State University, which was located at one of the edges of the capital. Thanks to arrangements made by Lya, he had ready access to the First Professor of the university. A very distinguished lady in her mid-fifties received him in her office. She said: "I am Ava. Elsewhere I would be called "The President", but we have done away with these grandiose titles, so that no one including me forgets that I am a professor first and foremost. Now that we have put that behind us, I like to welcome you to our university. I have been told by my dear friend Lya that you have already seen and learned a good bit of our country, and that she feels that you are searching for the heart of Shangri-La. Well, I believe that you have come to the right place, since it is here that our future generations enter adulthood, and it is here that they must find the spirit of the country, and learn what it means to be a good global citizen too." Ryan was curious about the method they used to achieve that goal and responded: "You are so right. I am very curious about how your system truly differs from systems elsewhere, so that you almost mold young people to be selfless and yet so caring about Life."

Ava: "We think that it is really rather simple. Children and young people are very innocent and caring by nature. They have no prejudices based on nationality, income, color, race, religion, beliefs etc. They are ready to make friends with the whole world. That includes animals and plants too. We adults often teach them or instill in them distorted values, often without meaning to, and often by our behavior and actions as examples. Here we simply try to build on the wonderful openness of the minds of our children. We try to teach them the totality first and foremost, and delay any kind of specialization as long as we can or rather till they choose to do what they like to do, and what they think they can do best. One may say that this way they become "jack of all trades and master of none". No, it is not so. They master the whole and concentrate on a part of that whole, while being aware of the whole at all times. I like to tell you a joke in this context. There was an international competition on the subject: elephants and there were four participants: a British, a German, a Frenchman and an American. The British went to Africa and wrote 'How to Hunt Elephants Efficiently', the German went to the library and wrote a seven-volume treatise titled 'An Introduction to the Life and History of Elephants', the Frenchman went to the zoo with a good supply of wine and wrote 'The Love-life of Elephants' and the American bought a pair of young elephants, took them back to USA and wrote 'How to Produce Bigger and Better Elephants'! I am sure that when the elephants heard the story they had a good laugh and said: "They should know better. We are actually like people. The most important thing about us is that we never forget anything and we mourn our dead". The point is that none described the elephants in their entirety successfully and instead, looked at them with a narrow focus. It is partly because of this that there is so much discord in the world."

Ava continued: "Coming back to our system, all the high school graduates are required to spend their first year at the university, actually away from it. They visit different parts of the country, stay there as guests of different families and pay for their expenses by doing various kinds of jobs. You may see this as an organizational nightmare. But it is not. Since generations have gone through this process, citizens at large are highly receptive to this program and they welcome the young boys and girls with open arms. This is not unlike similar guest programs instituted quite successfully in other countries for foreign students or the "Peace Corps" program instituted by the United States. Our professors, looking after the program, are aided but not replaced by today's technology to do the tedious book-keeping. The students are required to submit quarterly reports on their observations on some of the most important aspects of life, as they are being pursued where they are. These reports are discussed in depth when they return toward the end of the first year. During their three-year advanced training for graduation with a Master's degree, they are taught not only their own chosen area of specialization, if they wish to specialize, but an equal amount of courses which prepare them to live a 'Life' of fulfillment, and to provide selfless service to their community, the country and the world. The difference between our approach and that of many other countries may appear to be insignificant, and the knowledge base may not also be altogether different, however our emphasis on the whole and looking outwards beyond our narrow boundaries, can and should make a very significant difference."

Ryan listened intently but in his mind he could not readily accept all that the First Professor said. He asked: "Are you proposing to remake human beings, so that they care more about others than themselves, give up the tendency to acquire maximum wealth through their own enterprise, and thereby help maximize their country's GDP, even if resources keep getting scarcer, and air and water pollution exceed critical dangerous levels?" Ava replied: "No, we are not re-making anyone. It is extremely difficult to re-make once the die has been cast. What we are doing is known as "catch them young". Young minds are easily impressionable. Hopefully we are impressing on their minds the nobler instincts of humanity by taking advantage of the noble instincts that children are born with. Further, we grown-ups try our best to set examples which they can emulate. I remember a story in this connection. A man told his son to buy silver plates for himself, his wife and the children but only two earthen plates for his aged parents. The son complied but bought two extra earthen plates too. The astonished father inquired why he bought the extra earthen plates. The son replied: They are for you and Mom when you become old. Indeed selfishness does not pay, especially in today's world. Air-pollution does not distinguish between rich and poor. Neither do global warming, melting ice-caps, rising sea level, growing water shortages, growing desertification and dust-bowl effects. Regardless of all the wealth one may acquire it will be the same world that we will leave behind for our future generations, rich and poor alike. These are some of the rather easy-to-understand thoughts that we impress on the minds of our children."

Ryan asked: "How can you expect them to be selfless and yet so caring about 'Life'?" Ava replied: "There is no contradiction. To be able to help others one must be strong physically and mentally. Only then can they show others the way to be likewise. A strong mind can be selfless since it is already filled with what matters most, happiness born from well-being all around, and concern for the well-being of fellow human beings and that of the environment. There is immense joy in leading a life that sustains and even enhances both human environment as well as natural environment. We feel that true happiness cannot come from greed and an unending desire for ever-greater consumption that leaves one wanting a disproportionately larger share than that of others. You will hear this time and again in Shangri-La in many different forms and contexts. That's because our entire population is tuned to the concept and they support it with all their hearts. Would it be right to say that we need a break now? Let us have lunch and afterwards, I would like to give you a walking tour of the university."

As at the school before, the First Professor had invited a number of professors to join them at lunch. To Ryan's surprise, they had all brought their own lunch from home. This they shared between themselves and with him. The food was nutritious and delicious vegetarian. It included fresh vegetables and fruits raised by the students and professors on campus. He also found out that they all either walked or biked home. The university comprised one building, laid out somewhat like a fish-bone, with open spaces between the arms. The central spine was symbolically the entire world of knowledge from which different areas of specialization branched out. As one walked along the central spine, one was exposed to exhibitions of drawings, models and media projections of student work. Even though the building was largely single-story there was some provision for vertical as well as horizontal expansions. As Ryan had seen elsewhere in Shangri-La, there was abundant presence of solar panels and wind-turbines. The open spaces were largely used for agriculture. Both professors and students spent some time in raising some crops. Some space was devoted to experimental works, models and so on. The front end of the spine was the entrance, with bicycle parking and fruit gardens outside. At the far end of the spine was a large play area with a lake beyond, for swimming and other recreation on its shore. The First Professor took him to a number of schools within the university and let him meet both professors and students. Ryan was particularly interested in meeting the professors of the School of Medicine. The First Professor noted: "We call it the School of Health, since health does not always equate with medicine. In fact in our system it seldom does." Ava introduced Ryan to the Professor-in-charge of the School, who welcomed him. Before saying goodbye to Ryan, the First Professor invited him to give a talk to the students at his convenience. He promised to do so at a later date.

Ryan first joined the professors at the School of Health for tea. He then asked: "Why is yours not a School of Medicine?" One professor replied: "Simply put, medicine and health are not synonymous; one need not necessarily take medicines to be healthy. There are many aspects of health. First and foremost, we emphasize the importance of remaining healthy by being pro-active in preventing disease. We teach our students that the key to good health is proper nutrition and exercise, of both mind and body and not merely popping pills, when they are not necessary. Prevention also includes not being addicted to food, alcohol, smoking or drugs. In fact we have them practice what they learn in the classroom. Furthermore, we set a good example by practicing all these ourselves. Exercise need not be done in a gymnasium, using multiple gadgets. Everyone is involved in producing food and that itself is good exercise. Almost everyone walks or rides a bicycle for most commuting. They play group games like soccer, basketball and so on and participate in various physical exercises, including stretching, which children do instinctively and are also excellent for the elderly. People have their breakfast and dinner at home with the family. All this and also being with nature and having some quiet time, help nourish their minds. We reduce their interaction with television, computer and various media gadgets to a minimum and that too in a group and for specific purposes. There is no regimentation. Young minds need to be guided towards the positive and that is all we do. We teach them how food acts as an effective preventive and also curative medicine in almost all instances. Unfortunately, a conventional doctor almost never gets a chance to talk to people about these vitally important things. Conventionally, one visits a doctor only when one is sick and expects to be cured. One often gets cured but unless the root-cause is cured the disease often returns with vengeance. However, I must add that today, unlike in yester-years, excellent information on how to prevent disease in the first place is abundantly available, if one cares to pay attention to it."

Ryan asked: "Are you saying that prevention can solve all our health problems?" Another professor replied: "By no means. Prevention can possibly reduce the occurrence of disease, and even disabling accidents, by as much as fifty percent. For example, an elderly person who practices stretching exercises, walks some, and gets the right amount of calcium, is less likely to fall and have a hip-fracture. Also, it is little understood by the vast majority of people around the world, that a person practicing preventive measures, has a better chance of recovering from a disease, and that too sooner than a person who does not. There are also external factors, like air, water, sound and light pollution. Our students learn the benefits of improvement in these areas. Our doctors play a major role in guiding the society towards achieving these goals in co-operation with other major experts involved, like planners and administrators at various levels of Service. But we also teach our students how to cure when disease hits, as it does sometimes, in spite of our best efforts for prevention."

The professor continued: "We teach them that there are many systems available to treat a disease. Some are millenniums old and tested through thousands of trials. Unfortunately, these systems which are often very inexpensive and non-invasive, are often treated in some countries as voodoo or fake, and decried at every opportunity possibly by vested interests, which effectively make them unavailable to people. There are also many excellent modern medicines, though some have serious side-effects. Too often they are used almost exclusively, and can be very expensive, at least when they are first marketed. There are also excellent specialists, like surgeons who specialize in one organ of the body or another, and often use some of the most advanced technology. Unfortunately, the specialists often fail to see and consider the whole patient, and that can sometimes inadvertently lead to extremely serious consequences. We teach our students to be generalists first and foremost and till the end of the treatment, no matter how much they may specialize."

Another professor added: "We also teach our students to practice what they preach. A physician, who does not appear to be in good health and apparently indulges in unhealthy ways, cannot convince the patient of the efficacy of treatments he or she prescribes. This reminds me of a story. One day a lady brought her young son to a very wise man and urged him to advise her boy not to indulge in too many sweets. The wise man replied: "Bring him back after a month." When she took the boy back after a month the wise man asked the boy not to eat many sweets. The lady was surprised and asked: "But why didn't you tell him the same a month ago?" The wise man replied: "I used the month to give up my own habit of eating too many sweets."

Another professor chimed in: "Like in a few isolated countries, we let our students understand well that our business is the "health" of our people, and that "health" is not a business. In fact, healthcare is free for all in Shangri-La, like clean air and clean water are. Indeed we take great pain in keeping our air, water and yes, our bodies and minds in good shape. Learning about health is also free. Making these free saves us a good bit of potential costs."

Ryan asked: "How do you finance healthcare and learning about it?" The same professor replied: "Ryan, we really go back to the basics and ask ourselves, "Why must healthcare be very expensive?" My colleagues have already stated that we put a very heavy emphasis on prevention. We keep our environment as clean as possible and let nature embrace us everywhere. Nature provides us with an endless array of medicines, which one can grow even in one's own backyard garden, and our citizens do so. Such medicines have little or no side-effects. Often what nature offers us come in the form of delicious and colorful vegetables, fruits, roots, herbs and nuts. Since we do not consider healthcare as a business, we studiously shun any efforts to define a symptom as a disease. For example, we do not consider obesity as a disease and do not ask people to spend money on medicines or surgery to "cure" it. Have you seen obesity among people for whom walking is the rule, who do not sit in front of a TV or a computer for hours and do not eat lots of high-calorie or junk food? Likewise, smoking is not a disease to "cure" with medicines. It can be stopped very easily through resolve alone. We believe that these common-sense non-medical measures have cut our potential costs by an estimated 50%. We cover the other 50% with tax revenues. We let the private hospitals, clinics, doctors, pharmacies and insurance companies, from multiple systems, take care of the patients at any time that they are in need. Our National Service keeps the entire system accountable and sets standards of performance for these healthcare providers. While we allow profit-making, we also demand total transparency so that the community can see how the monies are being earned and spent. The National Service's prime task is to set standards for all the healthcare providers and administering payments to them. That's all."

Ryan wondered why all countries could not make healthcare free. But he had heard enough for a day and was also a bit tired. And always in the back of his mind the face of Lya shone like a serene and beautiful star, and he wanted to see her again soon. He thanked the professors for explaining Shangri-La's healthcare system and practices, and took leave of them, after receiving assurance that he could call upon them again. He started wondering if he could put his idle R.V. to some good use for Shangri-La, like to serve the cause of Health but could not decide readily. He wanted to discuss the possibility with Lya.

Chapter 9. To Deer Mountain :: Environment

He saw Lya after breakfast on Saturday, when she did not have to go to her office. His face lit up quite noticeably at the sight of her. She read happiness on his face and responded with a smile and her lotus-like folded palms. Ryan wished that she would open her heart a bit more. But even though there was no outward show on her part, he thought that he understood all the same, the subtlety of her feelings toward him. In a strange way, her reserved behavior made him feel even closer to her than if she had said too much. Presently she said: “Ryan, let us go to a different place this time. Our country has many hills, rivers, lakes and forests. And we are on the sea. You will be able to have a great panoramic view if we climb a hill. There is also an incline-lift for those who cannot walk or do not want to climb. Don’t worry. It is only about 250 meter high. We can ride our electric-bicycles or a mini-bus all the way to the base and then hike along a path to the top. It is not very far from here, only about twenty kilometers away. We can have a picnic or we can have a bite at the restaurant that is located very near the top of the hill. What would be your preference?" Ryan was in a dilemma. He liked her cooking very much but decided that it would be more relaxing for her if they ate at the restaurant. So he said diplomatically: "I cannot impose on your hospitality so often. Would you not rather take a break and let others do the cooking for us this time?" Lya was secretly pleased with his concern for her and replied: "You are quite a diplomat. We will have lunch at the restaurant."

As they rode along a narrow path, which followed a murmuring and glistening stream, and under a canopy of flower and fruit trees, Ryan remembered the narrow roads back home, which he drove along through national forests and by the streams. The only difference was that many cars tried to go fast and tail-gate impatiently and it was impossible to day-dream even in that paradise. Besides, his ex-wife did not care for such outings much. Lya did and it made a world of difference. Ryan found the ride exhilarating. The air seemed to sparkle, like the water in the stream and the shimmering leaves in the tree canopy. Most of all, he was enjoying the tranquility of the place. Occasionally they exchanged glances and smiles but none felt like spoiling the dream-like feel with words.

Presently, they reached the base of the hill, named Deer Mountain, because it was the home to hundreds of friendly deer. There was a small visitor center for conveniences; two young college students manned the center and welcomed visitors. Ryan spoke with them and found out that they were doing it as a part of their college work. Lya and Ryan started walking up the hill. Ordinarily one would take only fifteen minutes but they took their time in admiring the many birds, butterflies and the herds of deer, which seemed to play hide-and-seek with them. Ryan was always ready to help Lya with the climb, but to his disappointment and admiration, she managed quite well on her own. Eventually, they reached the restaurant near the top, went in and found a table with a sweeping view of the valley lying below. That was Nondon.

The restaurant was a one-story building, designed to blend in with the surroundings. It was deliberately situated near the top of the hill for sweeping views but not at the top itself, for that would be disrespectful to the natural profile of the hill. The building featured rough stone walls, stone floors and even a stone shingle roof, on which there was a wind turbine, solar panels and down-spouts for harvesting rain water. The walls and the ceiling were finished with wood-panels. The furniture was low and made of cane. The lighting was subdued, and it was synchronized with the level of light outside, for economy. There was an open terrace at a lower level, with gentle steps and a ramp leading to it. Ryan was very pleased. He was reminded of similar facilities back home. The view from the restaurant was quite breath-taking. What struck Ryan most was the well-defined boundary of Nondon and the extensive green cover within the city. There were other hills in the distance. In-between he could see almost endless agricultural fields, interspersed with fruit orchards and forest belts. A river meandered gently through the landscape. Hovering above it all there was the canopy of a shining blue sky with a few patches of cloud. As he looked around he felt like they were sitting in the middle of the work of a great painter.

They ordered vegetarian food, fruit juice and shared the colorful and aromatic dishes. Lya said: "Ryan, I wanted to discuss the all-important issue of environment today and that is partly why I selected this particular spot. Often when people talk about the environment they think of air-pollution, global warming and the like. We take a much broader approach, for we cannot achieve health unless we have a good environment. At the root of all our environmental problems lies excessive and obsessive consumption as though happiness comes from it. No matter how one cuts costs through efficiencies in production, it's a no-win battle, for un-satiable consumption eats up the savings rapidly. And as a result, non-replaceable resources get depleted as fast. Of course, we cannot stop consuming but we surely can rely as heavily as possible on sustainable consumption. The pressure is reduced considerably if we consume optimally and sensibly. That is good for our physical and mental well-being too.

Lya continued: "Here in Shangri-La our food and clothing come largely from plants of all kinds. They are renewable; they produce food using sun, soil and water, all of which are in abundant supply. We do not however take water for granted and waste it. Neither do we strip our hills of vegetation and let rainwater wash away top-soil. Our shelters can be built using materials like adobe and stone on one hand and trees and various plants on the other. Our energy needs, if we do not waste it or use excessively, can be satisfied well using wind, sun, geothermal energy, hydro-electric and ocean waves. That is a big "if", since most countries tend to misuse and over-use energy produced by fossil-fuel, whose supply is limited, and which emits greenhouse gases. Those in turn poison the air, produce acid-rain and raise global temperature. Why must we have day-light effect in so many indoor and outdoor places at night and why must we not see beauty in darkness too? Isn't it wonderful to gaze at the night-sky, in which stars shine like jewels and the Milky Way looks like a heavenly path? What inspired mankind through time immemorial is virtually lost to us if we turn our back to the serene beauty of night." Ryan was spell-bound watching the serene beauty just in front of him, and had no desire to break the passionate flow of her words.

Lya continued: "We have to acknowledge that our mineral resources are finite. They are increasingly hazardous and more expensive to extract, and when we process them to produce goods, there are many poisonous bi-products. The discharges pollute our air and water. As our consumption increases, we use up more and more land in various ways, like using up agricultural land and cutting down rain forests. Where do the animals go? Sadly, many of them go into extinction. We forget that if they go, we being a part of the animal kingdom, might follow them too. One can go on and on. Excessive consumption and condemnation of our own future go hand in hand. There is no if and but about it. What do you think, Ryan?"

Ryan, reflecting on his own disdain for materialism responded: "I am not a very articulate person, but I find the tendency to consume excessively very disturbing. In fact being repelled by it, I took to the road and finally reached Shangri-La and met you." Lya could not but sense the emotion in Ryan's voice and in his eyes but let him go on. Ryan continued: "Personally, I also feel that consuming without any concern for one's own true well-being, is a path to ruination in every possible way, be it in the form of obesity and disease or in the form of illusive power and wealth." Lya said: "Ryan, you are expressing it quite well. Carry on." Ryan: "I am beginning to put the pieces of the environmental puzzle together in my mind. I see how you are addressing the issue from all different angles, starting with small homes, tight-knit settlements, narrow roads for essentially small and human-power driven vehicles, emphasis on walking, frequent open spaces, use of natural sources of energy, vegetarianism, respect for nature and more, and very importantly, teaching children to value Life above all. To me it is beginning to make a lot of sense. Why can't all countries do likewise?" Lya replied with a mischievous smile: "Ryan, you are beginning to sound like a true Shangri-Lan. When you go back home they won't be able to recognize you!" Ryan: "Truly Lya, since I met you, I am not the same person anymore." She felt uncomfortable with the direction their conversation was taking.

She quickly responded: "You know Ryan, if other countries would place concern for the environment high up on their agenda, we would have a better chance for success, for our world is one unified ecosystem. We cannot have clean air unless others do too. We cannot have clean water unless others have it too. Global warming does not stop at our borders. Eating up all the earth's resources affect us too. We need to persuade other countries to optimize consumption for their own good as well as ours. That is one of the greatest challenges of our times." Ryan replied: "You are hinting at something that I feel like focusing on. This is one great cause, which today's clean-energy technology can really help us with, at a very reasonable cost and without harming the environment one bit." What Ryan just said touched a very sensitive chord in Lya's heart. She made a great understatement as she said: "Yes, this is our cause. But Ryan I hope that when you return home, you will remember all the causes, and let others know about them through your writings and speeches. I admire your quest to learn about Shangri-La. There is a lot more. People will ask you about many things and it is my great pleasure to help you in finding some answers. Ryan, you are a perceptive person and I am sure in your mind, you are linking it all together." Ryan did not say anything. He was still thinking about what Lya said a bit earlier: "Yes, this is our cause". Did she mean their cause or merely Shangri-La's cause? He wished that it was both.

They were so engrossed in their discussion that they almost forgot to eat. Lya said: "But to do all that you have to be strong. Now, better eat." They ate quietly, as they reflected on what they had just discussed. As they walked down to the base of the hill, Ryan admired the care with which the walk was made educative and enjoyable. Every now and then, there were tastefully designed signs, giving the names of trees and animals, which frequented the hill, and their pictures and brief descriptions. And there were occasional seats for resting and enjoying the sights and sounds. They saw many kinds of birds and animals. The hill reverberated with birds' songs and other creature sounds. It was like a concert in the air and so soothing. The exhibits at the small visitors' center at the base summed it all up. It also encouraged visitors to be respectful to the environment, and to volunteer their time to help maintain the ecosystem, and further, appealed for donations for the upkeep. Ryan and Lya happily responded. They noticed that other visitors did the same.

●

Chapter 10. Industry & Transportation

Ryan and Lya met again on Wednesday in the evening. Their meetings were by now fairly routine. They enjoyed each other's company a great deal. Ryan admired her wisdom, her uncommon willingness to teach a novice like himself the subtle ways of Shangri-La, and of course the charm of her personality. Lya in turn liked him for his eagerness to learn about her country in all sincerity, his respectful attitude to Shangri-La's unique ways and his subtle ways to let her know about his growing feelings for her. The last thought bothered her, for if he was planning to return, how would he cope with his familiar world back home? For now however, their feelings and thoughts remained largely hidden in their own hearts. They proceeded with their mission in the "business as usual" style.

Ryan observed: "Lya, You have told me a lot about how Shangri-La keeps consumption at an optimum level, but you have not told me what is produced here and if you export anything. I am not an economist but I do not see how Shangri-La can sustain itself, and offer free healthcare and free education unless it produces much more than it consumes." Lya responded: "I am not an economist either. I am a generalist, who has to think of the economy in the context of the well-being of the people. Remember, in this country well-being comes first. Here economic development is to serve well-being and not to blindly self-serve, often at the cost of the misery of a large segment of the people. For us, the well-being of all and not merely a few is to be attained. We do not place much value on GDP until and unless wealth is distributed fairly, and even more, unless the well-being of all our people is achieved and all are happy. The purpose of production needs to be considered before we decide about what and how. Of course we produce what we need for the nourishment of our own bodies and minds, the animals we keep and our soil. Also, we must produce for clothing, shelter and transportation."

Lya continued: "Production of goods and services serves another very important purpose. It enables full employment of our people, and finding happiness and health through work. Why? Because one needs to feel that he or she is making a direct contribution to the well-being of the country. We remember well the call made by the President of USA, John F. Kennedy: "Ask not what your country can do for you. Ask what you can do for your country." This is very much in the spirit of what we believe in. We deliberately try to achieve full employment. The social cost of unemployment is well-known, and yet most of the developed countries do not strive to attain full employment .They consider around 5% to 6 % unemployment acceptable for the sake of choice or competitive salaries, I suppose. We do not subscribe to that policy. We do not accept that any citizen of this country needs to be unemployed or poor, and we ensure that all our citizens have their basic needs fulfilled. There are two very relevant sayings: "You lose what you don't use" and "Idle mind is the Devil's workshop". I do not take these too literally. But we do not believe in "retirement". Except for extreme disability, a person can and should be able to work till he or she can. It helps them as well as the country."

Lya went on: "You may wonder how we can afford to have full employment. It is not that difficult if we go back to our value system and place Life above everything else, especially material possessions. The real question is, can a society afford to see many of its people unemployed without having grave consequences? Cost, as you know, is a relative thing. We cannot count cost of labor or giving employment to all, in isolation. We must take into consideration, the devastating social costs of unemployment. When one does that, the cost of mass production by machines or automation to replace people, or making some people work overtime to save on hiring others, turns out to be very high. Also the social cost of huge gaps between the incomes of various people is considerable. Our society does not respect or value ostentatious wealth or so-called luxury. Thus there is little incentive to have a large difference between wages, and hence we do not think in terms of a minimum wage. Why should there be an essentially discriminatory wage at all? After all, often it is our sons and daughters who earn some money doing work which is most labor intensive. Isn't it strange to think of white-collars having blue-collared children? In this context, I like to mention that we do not believe in slave labor in any form, including labor by genetically created sub-humans, and in using any kind of behavioral engineering on people, as advocated by some. We value work as a health-giving experience and do it to improve ourselves. The only work we do share with machines is what humans almost cannot do, or can do while risking their own safety. Also, by simply optimizing consumption on all fronts, private and public, we cut down all our expenses, including labor costs, considerably. We also save on health and environmental costs by not using fossil fuel to run our industrial machines. On a separate note, we do not produce and export anything, which in our way of looking at it, does not contribute to anyone's well-being including those who are not in this country. To do otherwise would be hypocritical. My dear Ryan, am I confusing you?"

When Lya ends like this, Ryan's confusion is twofold and it goes well beyond the subject that is being discussed. It takes him time to gather himself and respond. Ryan made an effort to say something: "Lya, I am confused but not in the ordinary sense." Lya mischievously responded: "I think I know what is extra-ordinary. But now, please pay attention to what I am saying instead of letting your mind wander in extra-ordinary confusion! May I proceed?" Ryan merely nodded in agreement. Lya: "As you may have guessed, we lean toward small-scale industries precisely because they are employment-intensive and can be managed by private enterprises utilizing small spaces and clean energy. Incidentally, would you believe that even in the most highly developed countries 99% of all industries are small-scale? Yet people mostly talk about the showy large-scale ones. We are also very particular that our industries are sustainable in the sense that they use inexhaustible and clean resources such as clean energy, converted into electricity, and renewable and or biodegradable materials. One positive by-product of our effort is that we have almost no waste and almost no greenhouse gas emissions."

Lya continued: "You may ask if we are talking about cottage industries. Yes, to some extent. But we are also very much in high-tech industries, including nano-tech, which could help us produce what we need, using ever-smaller amounts of material resources and energy. Our students and teachers are constantly doing research toward achieving our goals in this realm. They are constantly innovating. Interestingly, they are searching for alternatives to petroleum-based products even when the price of petroleum is comparatively low, since it is well-known, that in the end, petroleum is a limited and non-renewable resource. Admittedly, we cannot and need not produce everything that we need to use, because there are certain resources which we do not have, and there are certain products others can possibly produce better than we can. Thus we either buy those resources or buy the products. But before we buy either one, we make thorough enquiry about whether the products are being made in conditions which we find acceptable. We also check their accounts to ensure that the pricing and distribution of profits are according to the principles we believe in. We do not use any form of slave labor and shun any company which uses slave labor, and we lean toward those which use clean energy. This is one way for us to let others know about the principles of 'well-being first'."

Ryan asked: "Lya, you have been talking mostly about principles. Can you give me some examples of the kinds of goods and services that Shangri-La offers to other countries? Lya: "Ryan, I am so happy that I could hold your attention this long with a rather dry subject. It is a beautiful question. Of course, I shall be happy to mention some. Our most important export is not material goods at all. It relates to medical services. Many people come to Shangri-La to learn about our preventive healthcare methods. They stay here between one and two months, and experience the many steps we take toward preventive healthcare. Those include diet, exercise of both body and mind, socialization and being one with nature. They stay in the many inns, including Inn Jasmine. Perhaps you should consider doing the same. No, seriously, Ryan, you are doing much more than that. Sometime in the future we may have Shangri-La-based private enterprises operating Preventive Healthcare Centers in other countries too. We would do this to help others who cannot come and stay here easily. However their experience cannot be quite comparable to the experience that one would get by being in this environment. One of our big export items comprises frozen, canned and bottled health-giving food, which acts as conventional medicine. There is quite a bit of demand for it since we add absolutely nothing but what is needed to preserve it. No food colors, salt, sugar, fat, vitamins or spices. Essentially it consists of virtually raw food, which is packed very rapidly and still needs to be cooked to taste."

Lya went on: "We also export many different household goods like clothing, furniture and building materials, made of renewable materials like bio-plastics, ceramics, glass, wood, wool, bamboo, cork and paper. We are quite advanced in producing nano-structured and micro-structured materials and electronics. In essence we produce, use and export virtually all commodities and services which sustain our way of life. Let me give you some more concrete examples of another kind. We produce all kinds of small electric vehicles, starting with electric bicycles and even tricycles, electric cars , mini-buses and trucks and even a few big ones like electric trains, even though we may not make all the parts. Also, many foreign companies use our research organizations to do research on clean-energy, energy-efficient products, so-called alternative medicines, preventive healthcare and the like, in which we excel. And, would you believe it, we export vast amounts of clean energy itself, in the form of electricity. Ryan, have I given you a general idea of what we produce and export?"

Ryan replied: "You certainly have, Lya. I would say it is more than general. Yet I want to know more. During my travel through different parts of Nondon and Shangri-La, I have not noticed any industrial or office parks or even large shopping malls. I have also not seen any mega highways. Are there none? How do you manage without them?" Lya smiled and said: "Too many questions, Ryan. But I like your questions. They make me consolidate my thoughts. You will excuse me if I sometimes repeat what I may have told you some days or weeks ago. I do that so that we do not lose sight of our most important thoughts. Now back to your questions. Indeed you would not see industrial or office parks and large shopping malls, big parking lots and mega-highways, simply because we do not have them. You most probably know that in the good old days all different activities used to be together. People lived, worked, shopped, socialized, played, prayed, and did all else in one single walk-able and lively environment. They were aware of and cared about all that was going on in their community. Historically speaking, as industries and commercial activities became very large and often polluting, noisy, and congested, there was a move to separate them from residential uses, and from each other, into separate zones. This was done quite forcefully, particularly after World War II. Even within the residential zones there were sub-zones for different sizes and types, essentially separating the rich in their mega-mansions on mega-lots from the dense quarters of the middle-class, the poor or the young, who ironically could be their own children. The end-results were a disaster in urban living. Among them were long commuting, which was one of the most wasteful human activities, urban sprawl which ate up very large tracts of forest-land, and large asphalt spreads in the form of mega-roads, mega-buildings and mega-parking lots, which in turn created heat-island effect."

Lya explained: "By switching to people-intensive industries and commercial uses, high-density settlements, walking, bicycles and mini-buses for most urban transportation, and use of clean-energy almost exclusively, we essentially removed the justification for separate zones for different uses. So, in this country we place our industries and commercial uses within, or in the case of comparatively large ones, in close proximity of residential and other uses. In fact, we deliberately seek out opportunities to live and work under the same roof, as my parents and I do at Inn Jasmine. Of course if anyone wishes to place an industry, for example a food-processing unit, or a commercial unit like an inn or a shop in a rural area, one is free to do so. Please understand Ryan, we seldom, if ever, restrict anything. We simply create the conditions necessary for a vibrant urban life, and people find that those are to their advantage." Ryan simply said: "I do understand, since what you have told me just now fits in with your overall objective of putting Life and well-being above all else. And yet, when you talk about industries, the question of transportation naturally comes up. How do you move goods and people?"

Lya replied: "You are an excellent observer. Nothing seems to escape your attention. As you have seen already, our people use the most non-polluting and socially friendly modes of transportation, starting with walking, electric bicycles and electric mini-buses. How far and how fast can one go that way? Well, quite far, since our developments are compact, and not cut up by multi-lane highways, which cannot accommodate slow-moving vehicles and of course, any pedestrians. We seldom have any big box-like establishments anywhere, let alone in urban areas. As such, we hardly need any parking lots. As you have guessed, we do not put a premium on speed; why rush all the time? Why not enjoy the environment around, or even socialize while going places? Why shouldn't children be able to walk safely to their schools, instead of being bused? Why shouldn't grandparents be able to walk to a store holding their grandchildren's hands? Why do they have to depend on others for a ride? Ryan, again we value Life above all and to us movement is also an integral part of living: we need not rush always. Yes, for long distances we do use electric trains and when we need to cross seas and oceans we use ships and ultimately flights, one of which I may have to use when I visit you. Our trains are not superfast, since we do not see any point in wheezing past all the places, as if they do not mean anything to us. We do wish to interact with people and places as much as possible. Our industries use all the available modes as needed, and for the comparatively faster modes, we do have appropriate roads or tracks, which are often grade-separated to give priority to walking, biking and mini-buses." Ryan almost stopped listening when Lya said, "when I visit you". He said softly: "Will you really visit me when I go back?" Lya was lost for words. She was talking about transportation and did not realize that her chance utterances would be taken so seriously by Ryan. She lowered her eyes and remained silent. Ryan also did not want to embarrass her. He too remained silent for a while. Eventually he said: “You know which my most preferred mode is?” Lya thought she knew, but continued to remain silent. Ryan said: “Walking. Walking with you, surrounded by nature. When shall I have that privilege again?”

Lya replied with a smile: “You may have that special privilege only this Saturday, but it has to be a serious learning session nonetheless. Think of what we have left out. Very soon you will be all prepared for “graduation” on your knowledge of Shangri-La. By the way how is your writing on Shangri-La coming along? I can hardly wait for the day when it will be complete for publication, and I get the first choice to read the final draft, assuming that I shall have that privilege.” The very thought of completion brought a strange feeling in Ryan. His own life and what he came to study were becoming inter-twined. His own world was becoming full of Lya. He did not look forward to the completion of his “coursework”. He merely said: “Lya, all that you have told me so far is a noble concept, a concept which has been given real shape in Shangri-La. I would like to know about the system of governance of the country, and how it is sustained. And Lya, I am very much concerned about the defense of Shangri-La, where you live.” Lya was amused by Ryan's way of stating his concern for Shangri-La's defense. And yet, she was more than a bit touched by his worry about her safety. But as always she kept her feelings to herself and simply replied: "My dear Ryan, patience. You are asking me some of the most difficult questions. In fact, I do not know if I can answer all of them satisfactorily, for both our system of governance and system of defense are perpetually changing. But I shall try my best. It is getting late however. Let us meet again on Saturday morning. This will also give me a chance to gather my thoughts."

●

Chapter 11. To the Vineyards :: National Service

Saturday finally came. They met after breakfast, and rode their electric bicycles to a valley near Nondon. A good part of the valley was covered with vineyards. Lya took Ryan to a small cluster of rustic buildings, situated right in the middle of the valley. She said: "Ryan, I want you to see one of our small-scale industries; here we can taste some wine, and have our lunch too. But be careful. Don't get drunk! Apart from the winery complex, there is also a nice grove of trees just around the corner; it is a highly popular place. People come here to see the winery, have a nice lunch and relax too." Ryan was impressed by the warmth of the people who showed them around, the love and care with which they handled the bottles and the joyous atmosphere of wine-tasting, and finally the quality of food served for lunch. There was a sense of personal touch in everything. It was a most pleasant experience.

Lya opened the serious conversation. She said: "You were asking me about governance and defense. First, I like to tell you about governance. Of course we believe in democracy, which is a government "of the people, by the people and for the people". As you know, democracy comes in many forms. And it also needs checks and balances. We see often how the rule of the majority, or vested interests of the minority, can thwart even the best intentions behind democracy. Here we have one hundred percent literacy, meaning a lot more than the mere ability to read and write. Instead, it is being able to understand well the implications of our national policies. With that as our base, we take a two-pronged approach to minimize the problems commonly occurring in democracy, as far as possible. To avoid the concept of the governor and the governed, which sadly sometimes descends into "the oppressor" and "the oppressed", we have done away with the word "governance" altogether and replaced it with "National Service", "Regional Service", "Local Service", and so on. Our elected or appointed officials are not to forget that their job is to serve the people. In everything we do by way of service, we first and foremost consider our basic values, which are happiness and well-being of all of our people.

Lya continued: “We take minority rights very seriously. We define a minority through many different criteria, such as gender, color, ethnicity, age, physical handicaps and also beliefs. Our country is truly secular. Here it is not enough that decisions are made by the majority or even two-thirds majority. The majority vote on any national issue has to be almost unanimous or at least 95%, so as to include all minority interests. To attain unanimity can be difficult and time-consuming, but once it is attained it is a smooth-sailing there on. Even in our highest levels of service it is mandatory that all diverse segments of the citizenry and all diverse regions of the country are represented in a balanced manner. The measure of success of our country is what we call Gross National Well-Being or GNW. This is fundamentally different from the measure of Gross National Product. We do not subscribe to the belief that more is merrier. In fact we strongly believe that optimization can bring us more happiness and all-round well-being at an optimum cost. To make sure that we are on the right track we do run frequent surveys to identify the rare instances of unhappiness and lack of well-being and follow-up on their remedies with lightning speed. Our service policies are modified accordingly and often, but after explaining to the people the reasons. This is very easy to do by taking advantage of today's electronic media. I shall tell you about the other 'prong'. But do you have any questions for now?"

Ryan asked: "Yes I am sure that I have loads of them. For now, please tell me how the National Service is formed and how it functions?" Lya: "Well, let me see where to start. I suppose a good place to start would be our Constitution. In essence it spells out a set of principles, which are to assure well-being and happiness of all the citizens irrespective of race, color, ethnicity, gender, religion and beliefs. Our Constitution spells out the components of National Service as: The Well-Being and Happiness Council whose function is to define the goals of the Country, The Ministries including the Ministry of Well-Being whose function is to formulate policies toward fulfillment of the goals, and The Administration whose function is to implement the policies laid out by the Ministries. As I have mentioned a bit earlier, the Council, the Ministries and the various Administrations must include a fair representation of all the minorities. You may have noticed that the word "law" or "legal" is not an integral part of our

Constitution, for we do not believe that "law" can determine social outcomes like equality or quality. We do not believe that to be at the highest levels of National Service, we necessarily need legal or financial experts. Instead, we require that all the top and near-top positions be filled by those who have a minimum of a Master's Degree in Well-Being. Similarly we also require that to elect for any national position or to vote for a national issue one has to have a minimum of a Bachelor's Degree in Well-Being."

Ryan was surprised and said: "How can so many people have degrees in Well-Being? And if they do, how can they excel in other disciplines?" Lya replied: "Great question, Ryan. This is how we do it. We start teaching our children the essentials right from day one, thus for them to get an additional Bachelor's or a Master's Degree is somewhat like learning a second language. I am sure you know that in many countries or cosmopolitan cities, people speak four or five languages. So, for our children to learn about what is so important for their own lives and their country is no sweat. Where Shangri-La differs from many other democracies is that when the citizens elect or vote, there is awareness among them about what they are doing and why. Everything else becomes much simpler once people are aware. I like to add that we shun using the words, left and right, left of center, right of center, conservative, moderate, liberal, centrist, gone south meaning negative, gone north meaning positive, and so on. To label someone or a party in such terms stereotypes them, even though the words themselves are quite harmless. Human minds are not rigid. One's thinking on an issue can change over time or in different circumstances. In fact, we are more concerned about inflexible dogmatism on any issue. Also, one can be very conservative on certain issues and liberal on others. We are very conservative when it comes to our basic goals of well-being and happiness, but very liberal when it comes to researching for means to achieve them. To avoid financial burden on candidates for elected positions, to create an equal playing field, we do not allow using the electronic media to advertise image-building or image-destroying information. Instead we encourage the candidates to meet the electorate face to face and we provide them with all possible assistance to enable them to do so."

Lya continued: "One further note about "governance", we do not like to use the word “governance” at all, but since it has international significance we use it mainly for foreign relations as needed: we have no President, no Governor, no Supreme Leader, no Supreme Commander, no Prime Minister and no first family or first lady. We only have a Council and the Ministers to serve the Council. The term of all elected officials is limited to four years, with no chance for a second term. But to maintain continuity their terms are carefully staggered.”

Ryan said: “All this sounds so new and inspiring, I need to absorb it all gradually. Earlier, you said that this country took a two-pronged approach to minimizing the problems commonly occurring in a democracy. Before I get lost, tell me about the other ‘prong’.” Lya laughed and replied: “I thought that you had already forgotten about it. The other “prong” is something which one cannot legislate, and without which no amount of legalities will succeed.” Ryan was eager to know. He exclaimed: “What can that be?” Lya said: “This is a most difficult thing to express. It is highly subjective. It is not quantifiable and yet no less important than all the laws in the world. Simply stated, it is respect, empathy and concern for others, starting with one’s seniors, particularly one's parents, then all else, and nature including all the flora and fauna. It is also respect and concern for the inanimate objects, such as rivers and mountains, as it used to be common in all cultures in the bygone days."

Lya continued: "Sense of justice cannot be created through legislation. It is a matter of feeling. It needs to be inculcated among children through many subtle ways and through one's own examples. No matter how much the mass media denies it, it does play a major role in presenting exemplary or opposite behavior to children and adults alike. As such, we do not permit broadcasting any material, including advertisements, which are contrary to our national ideals or baseless rumors. As much as we believe in and allow freedom of speech and expression, we do not permit disrespectful behavior inherent in burning the national flag or effigies of people. We also avoid display of abusive behavior in real life. Fortunately for us, it is virtually non-existent in Shangri-La. To tell you the truth, I like you, because you seem to have an innate understanding of what I am talking about, and you are so respectful and considerate to me, I mean, to everyone." When Lya talked like this, Ryan was at a loss for words. He could not fathom if Lya was simply using a figure of speech, or giving away her deeper feelings in unguarded moments.

But his curiosity won over what he would have really wanted to say. He said merely: "Thank you Lya, for the compliments. How can I possibly be otherwise with you, I mean, anyone!" Lya laughed noticing Ryan's deliberate play of words, and took it in stride. She replied: "Alright. What next, sir?" Ryan was indomitable. He asked: "What if someone does something wrong. Do you send him or her to the jail?" Lya replied: "This is one of the most difficult issues to consider, particularly if the crime is heinous. However, we firmly believe that no child is born with a crime gene. Thus, society at large has to take responsibility for a person's crime. As mentioned earlier, we catch them young and prepare them to value Life above all, to respect and empathize with others, and not to fall for lowly gratifications. The latter is portrayed in many different ways, with apparent glory, in many countries and it leads to wrong expectations, disillusion and crime. We preempt with extreme care the very reasons for going astray. We optimize consumption so that everyone's basic needs are fulfilled. Everyone is employed. We maintain a naturally balanced gender-ratio among our people; and women, who bring us to this world and nourish us, are regarded even more highly than men. Our accounts are transparent and our income distribution is highly equitable. We respect family life and deliberately spend time together as a family. We respect nature and interact with it abundantly. Our air and water are clean. Also we try our best to cut out harmful influences and temptations, which could potentially lurk around the corners or quite openly under the guise of extreme freedom of speech or expression. There are potential reasons why a person may go astray. Earlier, I may have covered these points and more but what I am trying to say is that crime does not drop out of the blues."

Lya went on: "So, what do we do if someone still goes astray? We treat that person as misguided and take care of him or her in one of our Opportunity Houses. Depending on the severity of the case or situation, the individual may stay there or visit one. There we determine the cause of the unsocial behavior, take care of the mental stress he or she is under, and open the door to opportunities. Opportunity Houses are a combination of a hospital, a school and a home. Keeping with our respect for Life, and our belief in building up the positive, starting from the childhood, we studiously avoid any sense or semblance of punishment. We do not believe that punishment deters crime, or shall we say misbehavior. Capital punishment is something which has no place in our country, nor does a jail sentence in the conventional sense. In our experience, love, understanding, affection, trust and the like go much further and do the job, no matter how long it may take. After all, even a misbehaving person is the responsibility of the society at large."

Ryan was stunned by the audacity of the approach. After a long moment of silence he said: "Your approach is so beautiful, so humane. It is bound to succeed. I really mean it. Perhaps we can call it a day and head for home?" Lya readily agreed, but not before saying: "Ryan, once again I thank you for taking so much interest in our country and how it works. But so that you can take your mind off the serious matters a little, I would like to complete answering to your question tomorrow, that is, if you like. We will talk about protecting Lya, in case our country is attacked." Ryan felt a bit embarrassed by her remembering his concern for her safety in the context of the country's defense and yet extremely happy with her gesture to propose the back-to-back meeting, which they had never done before. Lya added: "Afterwards, we will immerse ourselves in our cultural activities, which we have almost neglected to include in our discussions." Ryan happily agreed.

●

Chapter 12. To the Castle :: Defense

The next morning, after breakfast, Ryan met Lya in the park, in front of Inn Jasmine. Lya said: “I am going to take you to an interesting place.” Ryan replied: “Alright, surprise me.” Soon she herself was pleasantly surprised to learn that Ryan already knew quite a few places in and around Nondon, taking advantage of the days when she was not “teaching” him. So it was not going to be easy to give him a surprise. But she did have one in store for him. It was in keeping with what they were going to talk about on this day: Defense. It was an old castle on top of a hill, overlooking the River Padma and the surrounding countryside around it. One could also see from this vantage point the distant coastline of the sea. The hill was located about one hundred kilometers from Nondon. They took an electric mini-bus from near Inn Jasmine. The unhurried ride with quite a few stops took an hour to reach the foothills, on the bank of Padma. The bus climbed along a narrow serpentine path up to an elevation of about five hundred meters and reached a flat courtyard in front of the castle.

It was a gorgeous day, but the air had a touch of chill in it. Presently, they joined other visitors and walked through the well-maintained castle. It had many large rooms, exhibiting ancient furnishings and décor. The guide explained the history of the place. The final exhibit was the armory. Ryan was fascinated. As the tour ended, they found themselves on a terrace overlooking the landscape. There was a restaurant adjoining the terrace. One could buy lunch, and enjoy it at a table on the terrace as long as one wanted. Ryan commented: "Surely you don't expect to defend your country from this castle." Lya laughed and said: "We have a whole regiment of valiant knights here, and they would defend the country with their lives. Would you consider joining the regiment?" Ryan was intrigued by the playfulness of his most charming companion. He had not witnessed this before. Seizing the opportunity he replied: "Yes, to defend the land where Lya lives I would." Lya blushed, and switched to the subject of defense as fast as she could.

Lya said: "Isn't it a shame that even Shangri-La, which does not aspire to be rich and powerful, has to still think of defense? You know Ryan, it makes me sad when I think of the great waste nations make in preparing for war. I wish that instead of spending hundreds of billions for war, they would spend the same in friendship efforts. In the prevailing atmosphere that remains only a wishful thinking only. Or, does it? We find that there is a concerted international effort to eliminate nuclear, biological and chemical weapons and to negotiate for peace in the face of threats. For good or worse, countries are increasingly resorting to economic competition instead of cold or hot wars. They are looking for resources elsewhere when they do not have them, or do not have enough of them, and yet need them to satisfy their growing appetite for consumption. We view this as the root-cause of wars. Today, the new threat is from within. It is largely a result of excessive consumption by a small segment of the society, rising income gap and grossly uneven income distribution."

Lya continued: "In Shangri-La, we start with our values, the most important one being valuing Life above all. We consume optimally, and live within our means. All our people are employed. We distribute work and material wealth as equitably as possible, while depending largely on people's own initiatives. And above all, we are happy. Thus we have internal security. We do not attack any country. We actively engage in sending our boys and girls abroad for better understanding of other people, and making friends with them. We also invite exchange students, faculty and researchers from other countries, and immigration by those, who can make positive contributions to our country. We freely import what we do not have, and export what we specialize in. All these measures are designed to develop mutual trust, and a stake in the well-being of this country and that of others. We believe that there has to be a reason for an attack, and we studiously try to eliminate the potential reasons for that to happen. Fortunately, there is growing weariness world-over about war. It is no wonder, that more and more minds are finding our ways to be not only sensible but the only ones which the entire world can use to solve the growing problems. The list of problems include global warming, resource depletion, air and water pollution, famines, slavery, deforestation, floods and species-extinction. But what happens if all our efforts to avoid war do not work?" Ryan asked: "Yes, Lya, what if some country still attacks Shangri-La? I am sorry but I cannot take my mind off the possibility of any danger to you." Lya replied: "You are simply crazy."

She went on: “Don’t worry. Nothing is going to happen to me. We extend the olive branch to all, but at the same time, we also take reasonable precaution so that no country is tempted to attack us. For this, we use the most sophisticated technology that is available today, and innovations which our bright scientists are constantly working on. As you can well imagine, with the use of innovative technology, preventing attack on our soil is becoming easier and easier all the time. In fact, there are no limits. I am not in a position to discuss any more details. Ryan, one of our best defenses is in the mind of the person sitting right by my side. Your book and talks will hopefully make people aware of a better way to go about the problems. Your work will be supported by the fact that we must live in harmony with nature and with each other, for Life is valuable as it is beautiful.” Ryan was overwhelmed by her show of confidence in his humble self. He said: “I am only an insignificant person but your confidence inspires me to rise to the occasion. I promise that I shall do all in my ability to protect you, and to protect Shangri-La.” She could feel the emotion in his voice, but pretended not to notice it.

They finished their lunch quietly and walked down the hill, along a pedestrian trail, that generally followed the road. Lya said : "You know Ryan, when I am surrounded by nature and see the sun shining through the shimmering leaves and hear the birds singing, I feel mesmerized and I wonder why we all do not care to feel the gentle touch of Mother Nature at all times. Why do we wage wars against her, cut down trees, destroy the habitats of these beautiful creatures and let rain wash down the soil? Why do we wage any war at all? The world is so beautiful. Why don't we live in harmony with one another and with Mother Nature?" She went on like this, as if she was talking to the whole world as her audience. Ryan did not want to interrupt her thoughts. He merely said: "Lya, I feel the same way as you do. I think that Shangri-La will show the way to the rest of the world. I don't know if humans are inherently violent but there has to be two sides in any human mind. Your way must appeal to most minds and will bring out the best. There is no alternative. Is there?" Lya replied: "Ironically, the entire humanity would unify in no time if the whole world would face an imminent danger, like a large asteroid in collision course with the Earth or a tsunami hitting the coasts of all countries at the same time, or even the threat of an imminent alien invasion. Yet the threats that the entire Earth is facing today are very real, the only difference being that they are hurting us not in hours or days but over decades or more. We go on pretending that they are imagined, and go back to our in-fighting as though our narrow self-interests are what really matter. Ryan, it is said that "the pen is mightier than the sword". I hope that you will prove it, again and again."

Presently, they found themselves back on the bank of the Padma. There were small electric motor launches, which were ferrying people to the other bank. As Ryan was in no hurry to return to Nondon, and since it started drizzling a little, he suggested to Lya that they take the ferry ride. Lya readily agreed and off they went. Ryan noticed how happy and relaxed the passengers were. He struck up conversations with a few, and found out to his amazement, how well-informed they were about their own country and also about the rest of the world. He reflected on the fact that in his own land few cared to know about other countries. He thought perhaps he could make an effort to change that some. The day was nearing the end and they decided to return home. Lya promised to see him on Wednesday again.

●

Chapter 13. To a Community Center :: Beliefs

After they met in the evening, they had their usual cup of tea at a restaurant in a nearby square, and later took a leisurely walk. Presently, they were in front of a Community Center. Lya asked: “Would you like to visit it? I don’t believe that you have done that yet.” Ryan readily agreed. While inside, he was truly surprised by the array of facilities provided, in this consumption-conscious country. There was a library, a television-viewing room, an exercise room with some easy-to-use equipment, a room with several board games, several lounges where people could meet and also hold discussions, and a fairly good-size kitchen. Ryan remarked: “This is quite a community facility.” Lya replied: “We are largely outdoors people. But we have a few all weather facilities like this one, so that people can meet even in inclement weather. We encourage social interaction in all possible ways. It’s good for our minds. Also it brings people closer together. Now, let me show you something else.” He followed her as she led him upstairs. There was a lobby and it had subdued lighting. They removed their shoes and entered a very dimly-lit large circular room with a white vaulted ceiling and white walls. The floor was carpeted in white, and there was a low-rise bench along the periphery. Very gentle music, almost echoing the sounds of nature, was playing. Ryan immediately knew that this room could be meant for only one purpose: meditation. Both Lya and he sat on the bench. There were a number of other people, yet there was complete silence. It did not matter what beliefs were held by those present. They must have been feeling oneness with the Supreme. The two came out after some time in silence.

A few minutes later Lya said: "You may be wondering why I showed you the special room upstairs. The other day, when we talked about defense, I hesitated to mention a very important point with some implications for defense also, because it is a highly sensitive and seemingly charged issue. That unfortunately relates to religion or belief. Why unfortunately? Because, it has been a prime source of strife between nations and even within nations. A religion or a belief, by itself, is ennobling. The human mind has searched for meaning in all natural and apparently supernatural happenings, and also reflected on his or her own mind, from time-immemorial. Perhaps this is the only aspect that separates humans from all other animal species. Though the essential message of all religions and beliefs has been love for fellow human beings and one Supreme Being or Force, the so-called extremists, and at times, the vested interests, have often distorted this essence for their perceived advantage. They have waged wars in the very name of religion or sometimes discriminated against, punished or tortured those who disagree with them. They all profess to believe in one Supreme Being or Force and that all, including the flora and fauna, are created by the same One. Yet, they are fiercely intolerant of others' making the same claim and reaching out to that Being or Force in their own ways. They even assert that their Supreme Being or Force is the only one or the best one, and their way is not only the best but the only real one, the others' being "false". This is somewhat like calling one's mother in his or her own language and fighting over whose mother and whose way of calling is superior or real. Of course, mother has no problem in being called by different names and loves all her children irrespectively."

Lya went on: “In Shangri-La our National Service is strictly secular. We allow all beliefs as long as one makes no claim that one’s belief is the best or superior to someone else’s. This is consistent with our over-riding policy of allowing maximum freedom of speech and expression so long as it does not threaten someone else’s. We do not believe in extremes, since they have a way to hurt somebody. We encourage people to participate in others’ practices. People love it, for they find that most of others’ practices are also full of nobility and joy, like their own. Again, in keeping with our policy of allowing freedom unless one’s freedom threatens another’s, we discourage all such displays, as would offend some. This give-and-take works well and keeps away extremism from our land.” Ryan was quite amazed by Shangri-La’s very broad, thoughtful and humane approach to a most delicate issue. He said: “Lya, I feel reassured by your approach.” Lya replied: “You are near “graduation” in your quest to learn about this country. As promised earlier, we will henceforth immerse ourselves in our cultural activities.” Ryan was delighted, and yet he felt a tinge of sadness for he knew that before long he would not have Lya to tell her about Shangri-La, and that he would be pretty much on his own, to complete his account of the discovery of this very unique country and her uniquely humane ways. He merely nodded in consent.

Chapter 14. To Shangri-La Plaza :: Culture

On Saturday, they met in the afternoon and rode their electric bicycles to Shangri-La Plaza. Ryan had been here before to see where Lya worked. But today was so different. They were not going to talk about how the country functions. Today they would lose themselves among the people, who were there just to relax and have fun in the many ways that the Plaza made it possible. Meandering through the entire Plaza was a lake with a wide path around it. In and around the Plaza there were museums, gardens and fountains. Some museums were very special. There was an entire museum on Health. There were others on Beliefs, National Service and Environment. Then there were museums of Arts, Sciences, Archaeology and more. All were hands-on wherever and whenever possible. The facilities were sometimes inter-connected to emphasize the overlapping of the subject areas. There was also a well-equipped Theater and an Open Air Theater. There were many mobile food stalls, and abundant places to sit in the sun or in the shade of trees. And, there were people---men, women and children---in festive attires---happily moving from place to place or simply sitting and relaxing. Some played board games at the many tables placed throughout the plaza. What greatly impressed Ryan, was that there were also various buildings housing the Ministries around the Plaza yet there was no attempt to impress the people with grandeur. It was as though to reassure the citizens that the Ministries were at their service and not above them instead. The Plaza symbolized Life, the act of living, by the way opportunities for multitude of activities were provided for all.

Ryan was particularly interested in visiting the Museum of Health. He found it both great fun as well as educational. An enormous transparent model of a human body showed its various components and taught how it functions. There were even rides through enormous blow-ups of different parts of the body. One could see the many different types of food, where they came from, their effects on the human body, how they helped one heal, and even how to cook and eat properly. Large and dynamic models, showed how a body reacts to various exercises. Some showed even how the various organs of the body respond to deep breathing. They went through many such experiences and played with some of the hands-on switches. Lya often laughed. This was music to Ryan's ears. So he looked for all opportunities to make her do exactly that. Ryan also took a keen interest in visiting the Museum of Beliefs, assuming that it would be rather difficult to depict what was so abstract. He was surprised to find out that, small places for prayer and meditation or discussions existed, next to the main exhibitions on the various religions and beliefs, which formed the central axis of the Museum. The small spaces replicated the traditional places for the respective activities. Visitors could learn about the different religions and beliefs by simply participating in their chosen areas. Also they could get enough information to learn more in the future. No one laughed here but there were faces which radiated inner happiness.

By now, Ryan was getting hungry. Lya sensed it. She led him straight to a mobile food stall. She ordered for both, for she knew well what Shagri-Lan foods he liked to eat. Ryan had long since given up on being surprised by her ability to read his mind. They sat at a table under a delightful canopy, and debated what they would do next. The pleasant murmurs of the nearby fountain seemingly joined the conversation, and urged them also to be playful like the splashing water. As if to oblige, they headed for a large and very colorful carousel playing the music of Johannes Strauss. They felt youthful and jumped on two horses. As they went up and down and round and round, Ryan felt that he was dancing with Lya. He could hardly keep his eyes away from her face glowing with childlike delight. She cast a few glances at him and waved gently. Tough for him though, he could not fathom her mind. Yet he felt as though she was very close to him. After leaving the carousel, they took a walk around the lake. Presently, they came upon a group of young artists and sculptors. They were doing live painting, sketching and sculpting. People were watching intently and many were buying too. A few artists were making sketches of the visitors. After asking for her permission, Ryan requested a very talented young artist to make a sketch of Lya. He obliged and soon produced an exquisite life-like likeness of her. Even though Ryan had taken her photos, this sketch was very special. She accepted it happily as a gift from this very special student of hers.

It was getting dark. Well-shaded lights were soon turned on and their reflections in the lake created an almost hypnotic air. Children were riding small electric carts and giggling abundantly. Parents and grandparents were having a time of their life pursuing them. People were also gravitating toward an amphitheater in front of an open-air stage. As darkness set in well, a show of beautiful dances and heart-warming music began. Ryan and Lya sat on a wide step and enjoyed the show under the canopy of the star-studded sky. They lost themselves among the delightful people of Shangri-La.

●

Chapter 15. Ryan Proposes

On the following day, Ryan and Lya met in the evening on the banks of River Padma, which Ryan had seen before from the terrace of the castle. They had made reservations for a dinner cruise on the river. This was going to be the last of their cultural experiences, before Ryan would leave for his homeland. They were sitting facing each other by a window. A single rose adorned the vase on the table. Gentle music was being played by a band. They both looked a bit sad, perhaps thinking of the same thing. They had grown to like each other's company. Now it has to end: they had to go their own ways. Very discreetly, Ryan picked up the rose in front and extended his arm toward her in offering the rose. Seemingly Ryan wanted to say something, but did not know how to put the words together. He made a desperate effort: "Lya, I want to say something but I am lost for words. But I must, as I may never get this opportunity again." Lya made it easier for him: "My dear Ryan, what is it that you are finding so difficult to tell me?" Ryan: "Lya, I am not the same person whom you greeted at the Inn many months ago.

Perhaps, without realizing it, you have made a new person out of me. I find it extremely difficult to stop everything now. I find it too difficult to accept the thought of being away from you. Lya, I love you, love you very much. I cannot imagine being away from you and living without you. Oh Lya, may I ask you to be with me for the rest of our lives? May I have the honor of having you as my beloved wife?" Lya put her hand very gently over his just for a moment, and almost whispered: "Oh Ryan, I am so honored. You do know by now that I have become fond of you too. But how can I accept your very emotional proposal, knowing that you will go back to your homeland very soon and also, without the acceptance of you by my parents? You know that I cannot accompany you, for I love and believe in the ways of my country and I shall wither away if I move. Can you solve all this for me?" Ryan replied: "Yes I can. I shall not leave you. I shall not go back, if Shangri-La lets me stay. I shall complete my book, right here." Lya: "That's so sweet of you. I am truly touched by what you have just said but you will still have to receive my parent's blessings before their daughter can accept your proposal." Ryan: "But how do I do it? Please tell me". Lya smiled shyly and said: "I have taught you so many things but I could not possibly teach you how to ask my parents for the hands of their daughter. Could I?"

Lya couldn't sleep that night. Neither could Ryan. He could hardly wait for the opportunity to see Lya's parents, Leon and Maya. He did not know what to tell them. For once Lya would not help or perhaps she herself did not know what to say. He also did not know if she would mention anything about last night to her parents. Women could be so mysterious, he thought. All she said was that she was fond of me. But what more could she say? Back home things would be so different. Acceptance by parents would be the last thing to worry about. Thoughts were literally swirling through his mind and he could hardly wait to vent them.

Eventually morning came, as it always did . It was sunny and cheerful. This elevated Ryan's spirits and gave him the confidence that he badly needed. At breakfast, he glanced at Leon and Maya to gauge if they knew anything about last evening. No, they showed no sign of it. He mastered all the courage he could, and after other guests had left, approached Leon with folded hands. He asked: "Where is Maya?" She overheard him, peeped in and said: "What can I do for you, son?" Ryan folded his hands again in greeting and said in a shaky voice: "Could I have the privilege of seeing you both tonight when you are free?" Since Ryan had never made such a request before, they were both surprised. Maya said: "Of course. Please come to our private quarters at the inn itself at about eight in the evening and join us for tea." Ryan accepted. Again started a seemingly endless wait.

But evening finally arrived and a nervous Ryan showed up at the door to the private quarters of Leon and Maya. They greeted him with warm smiles, and asked him to take a seat in their living room, which was covered with mats like his own guestroom was. It was sparsely but tastefully furnished. Even though Lya also lived with them, he assumed that she would know about his visit and its purpose, and would go out to avoid being present at this very delicate meeting. Maya served tea and some pastries. After some moments of silence, Leon asked him: "You must have something important on your mind. What is it son?" Maya joined the conversation: "Is everything well with you? We know that you are doing a study of Shangri-La and that Lya is working with you on the project. Is she being of much help?" Ryan couldn't hold back any more. "Yes, yes, she has been of more help than I could ever imagine. But please forgive me for saying what I am about to say. She has not been working with me. It has been the other way around. She has been teaching me all about this great country, with the greatest sincerity. What she did not realize was that, in the process I was gradually transformed. Now that the Study is complete, I find it almost impossible to tear myself away from your most gracious daughter. And, please forgive me if I am being awkward in saying it, I most humbly ask you both for giving me permission to have her hands in matrimony."

Leon and Maya were taken aback. Maya asked first: "Have you asked Lya?" Ryan replied: "I have, last evening, and she said that I must get your permission first." Maya: "Son, if she has said that, she must be very fond of you. We have been seeing you for months, and we do know that unless she was fond of you she would not spend so much of her time with you. We like you too. But please do understand that there are many problems which you two young people may not anticipate. You will be going back soon to your country and may even forget her. She will not be happy being away from Shangri-La." Before she could even complete her sentence, Ryan said: “But I have no intention of going back. I want to stay here forever.” This time Leon said: “We appreciate very much what you are saying, my son. But we feel that you must make sure that you are not merely infatuated. Marriage is a life-time commitment, to take care of each other with love and care forever. Thus, we think that, it is best for now that you go back to your country for some time, in order to be absolutely sure that you are truly prepared to marry her. Son, we hope that you will understand. We want you both to be happy. A little patience would not hurt.” Ryan remained silent for a moment and replied: “I understand your point. I am not merely infatuated. I truly love your daughter and I am very much prepared to marry her. But I shall do as you wish and solemnly promise that I shall return”. As he was saying this, tears welled up in his eyes. Through his tears, he bade them goodbye.

A heart-broken Ryan felt lost. He could not face Lya the next day, and started preparations to go back. She also did not come to him. At the daybreak next morning, the sky became increasingly dark and gloomy . It started raining, as if on cue, to reflect the utterly pensive mood of the two minds. Ryan pushed on nonetheless. As he was finally ready to leave, Lya showed up quietly, touched his hand for a moment and said softly: "I could not bring myself to coming earlier. You will understand why. Please don't be disheartened. I know my parents well. They are our well-wishers. They are doing what they think is best for us. Oh Ryan, don't forget me. You mean much to me; you mean all to me." Lya's voice choked with emotion. Ryan whispered: "No, I shall not, my darling, I shall never forget you. I shall carry on with our mission even when I am away from you. You will be in my heart every moment." He could not say any more. Lya said: "You will take care of yourself. Won't you?" Tears welled up in her eyes. She did not want Ryan to see her cry. She touched his hand once more, and without saying a word, she gently walked away. Rain kept falling. Unseen, she waved till Ryan's RV disappeared around the corner of the square in front of Inn Jasmine. With it, she felt, her whole life just drove away into uncertainty. Rain kept falling.

●

Chapter 16. Stranger at Home

Ryan made his trip back home as fast as he could. What he had enjoyed seeing while coming to Shangri-La, could not hold his interest now even for a moment. He missed Lya with all his heart and felt an ache deep inside. Tears welled up in his eyes often. Even though he felt tired inside, he pushed on through many countries till he reached his home, his condominium in a high-rise building. But he felt as though he had left his heart behind. He missed his room at Inn Jasmine and missed all that was Nondon. He missed Lya beyond words. It took him many a days to regain a sense of normalcy, if one could call it so.

One day he paid a visit to his parents, who lived in a high-end development built exclusively for seniors. His siblings also joined them. He told them about Shangri-La, and how the entire country valued Life above all. He also told them, how they achieved happiness through health, optimal consumption, full employment, equitable distribution of wealth, being secular, avoiding extremism and leaving no one but no one behind in any aspect of life.

He further told them about adopting National Service in place of governance, having Opportunity Houses in place of prisons and defending the country essentially through friendship initiatives. And of course, he told them about Lya, how she combined uncommon grace with superior wisdom, and his plans to marry her. Their response was a mixture of disbelief on one hand and viewing him as different from themselves on the other. But about Lya, they were non-committal and said little. Ryan felt very uncomfortable, and took leave of them early.

Suddenly he had a strange thought. He was a stranger in his own home! But he would not let his feelings keep him away from his newly-found mission. He must push on with completing the book. And he must do much more. He would live up to the expectations of Lya. In his mind he resolved to start a new foundation, and devote to it, all the resources he had. Day and night he thought what to name the foundation. He considered 'Shangri-La Foundation'. But then that might sound too localized. What Shangri-La stood for was much larger than itself. It stood for 'Life' above all. Why not 'Life-Above-All Foundation'! He thought that that was a very broad umbrella, and under that all that Shangri-La stood for could be brought out well. He settled on 'Life-Above-All Foundation'.

Whenever he would get an idea, he would excitedly call Lya and if only she would get equally excited, he would follow up on it. It was a partnership and what was more, he felt that this way he stayed close to Lya, even during his "exile". Presently, he called his lawyer and got the thing moving in top speed. He used all the social media to spread the word and attract like-minded people, for he knew that ideas espoused by Shangri-La were not limited to the people of that country alone, and that there was a large following of similar concepts in every country in the world. He knew that Shangri-La was unique in that it had followed through those great ideas in building up a country, which valued Life above all, and everything else followed from there: yet she had avoided any kind of extremes. The real test was that it worked, as he himself had witnessed firsthand. The response he received, to his reaching out via the social media, was overwhelming. Before he knew it, there was a group of people, who expressed their desire to work with him for the cause, in his own city. He knew that to convince people that Shangri-

La really worked he had to also present the ideas in person, supported by photos and videos, to whosoever would listen. Thus, with the help of volunteers, he organized numerous conferences, podcasts and also live lectures to educational institutions and community organizations throughout the country.

While all this was going on and eating up his energy, he also worked on the book. He started to neglect sleeping, and worse, having health-giving meals or any meal at all on some days. Through it all, he never failed to communicate with Lya, who was proud of his achievements but unaware of the price he was paying in the process. Before long he completed his book titled: “Shangri-La. It’s Real”, dedicated it to Lya, and sent her the very first copy. He was happily walking back to his condominium after mailing the book, when suddenly he felt very dizzy. He desperately looked for a place to sit. There was none in sight. The whole world closed in as if, in broad day light, and he collapsed on the sidewalk. He barely could make out what was going on around him as help arrived and he was moved to a hospital. Several days later, he regained consciousness. When he opened his eyes, wondering where he was, he saw the anxious faces of his parents and siblings. As he came back to his senses fully, his sister uttered: “Ryan, you gave us a real scare and we are relieved to see you recover. If you will allow me, we have a most pleasant surprise for you. Now close your eyes again for a moment.” When he opened them again a familiar musical voice whispered in his ears: “I have come to take you back home. My parents send their blessings. And I have already received the blessings of your parents.”

●

Part 2

Chapter 17. Affirmation of the Mission

Lya, upon learning about Ryan's being gravely ill made a swift decision that Ryan and only Ryan could be her rightful partner in life. She could not live without Ryan and she knew too well how much he cared for her and needed her. She spoke with her parents, but little required to be said. Her loving parents knew well their daughter's mind and urged her to travel to Ryan's home country, Freedomland, and be at his bedside as quickly as possible. They took an electric bus and saw her off at the airport. Ryan's parents and siblings were looking forward to meeting her and eagerly received her at the other end. If they ever had even an inkling of doubt about this woman of whom Ryan spoke so highly, her very sight turned them into converts. Having laid their eyes on this very beautiful woman with uncommon poise and a very intelligent face with sparkling eyes, they fell in love with her almost immediately. Lya, on her part, had heard so much about his family from Ryan that she felt as though she knew them all well. She felt right at home almost in an instant.

Lya and Ryan decided that even though they would register their marriage in Ryan's home town and hold a reception for the family and friends, the actual marriage ceremony would take place in Nondon and it would be their home after they were married. These were not whimsical decisions. Ryan would not even think of uprooting his very dear Lya from Shangri-La, for he felt that she, would wither away if that would happen. He himself grew to believe in and like Shangri-La and all that the country stood for. He had not forgotten the common cause that they talked about a long time ago. Their mission would be nothing less than whatever they could do to make more Shangri-Las come into being throughout the world. They decided that to accomplish their goal it would be best to make Shangri-La their base, their home, for there they practiced what they preached and that too, most successfully. Indeed there the vast majority of the citizens were happy. Ryan would bring to the effort his intimate knowledge and understanding of the developed world in one of which he was born and the developing world, to both of which he had travelled extensively when he was looking for a place where his mind's restlessness would ease if not cease altogether. Intuitively they both felt that it would be easier to shape the developing countries in harmony with their ideals, since those were naturally looking for and experimenting with new paths to follow, but developed countries would be a different matter altogether.

True to her way of doing things, Lya told Ryan, "We must discuss our plans with your parents and seek their acceptance". Ryan replied, "Here in Freedomland grown-up children do not generally consult their parents about anything, let alone the most important matter of where we may settle down after our marriage". But Lya was not persuaded. She insisted in her great wisdom, "Ryan, what you are saying may be true but they would expect their would-be daughter-in-law from Shangri-La, to do things differently. They love you and I already know that they love me too, perhaps more than they love you. Don't they? We must not do anything to hurt their feelings. Would we?" Ryan could not face up to her indisputable argument. He was secretly pleased that Lya knew that she had conquered his parents' hearts. So, they discussed their plans with not only his parents but with also with his siblings. Even though Ryan's parents were hoping that Lya would prefer to live in Freedomland, they also sympathized with their noble mission and agreed that they could achieve greater success with it with Nondon as their home-base. Ryan's mother gave voice to their feelings by saying, "We are happy that you have even bothered to discuss the matter with your elderly parents. Lya, I suppose that we must thank you for that. We are also happy that our nomadic son is even thinking of settling down. Now, as much as we would have liked you two to stay here we do understand why you wish to go back. Let it be so, but you both must promise to visit us at least once a year and spend some quality time with us." The soft-spoken father merely nodded his head in agreement. As for Ryan's siblings, they were too overjoyed at the prospect of their brother's forthcoming marriage and having a remarkable lady like Lya as their sister-in-law. They even wondered loudly if Lya had any sisters. Nevertheless they looked forward to visiting Shangri-La. While Ryan and Lya sought to get their marriage registered they got busy preparing for a fitting reception.

Lya was quite overwhelmed by the pomp and pleasure of the occasion. Ryan's parent's imposing home on the golf course was decorated lavishly. Seemingly innumerable guests came wearing their best tuxedos and evening dresses. Ladies vied with each other for attention. Appetizer plates whisked through the gathering like flying saucers. Champagne flowed. Lya merrily raised her glass in a toast made to the just-married couple and charmed all the guests with her most elegant beauty. Dinner and dance with violins playing in the background followed till late in the evening. Even though she did not show it she felt a bit uneasy having been unaccustomed to the grandeur that enveloped her. Ryan's understanding presence let her take it all in stride.

With the festivities behind them Ryan and Lya set out for returning to Nondon. This time they resorted to a slower mode of transportation, namely a train ride. As the train moved through Freedomland, Lya was amazed to have glimpses of a world, which was very different from Shangri-La. She had seen a bit from the air, as her plane was approaching to land. What caught her attention most was the largeness and looseness of the developments she had flown over and now they were passing through. In Shangri-La almost everything was compact and towns and villages had distinct edges. But here nothing seemed to be defined. Everything was big and seemingly made for the scale of fast-moving cars and monstrous trucks. There seemed to be no boundaries, no sense of containment anywhere. There were endless expanses of asphalt with few trees if any around. She did not see anyone biking, let alone walking. Ryan sensed her bewilderment and merely told her reassuringly, "My love, hopefully we can bring about some changes to such scenarios. I have been thinking where we can start and how our efforts can bring the best results within the shortest possible time. This is our cause. Remember, you said that once, seemingly long time ago? I have not forgotten it. To my ears it had a double-meaning." Lya smiled. Yes. She remembered. Did she realize at that unguarded moment how her chance utterance, with the implicit double-meaning would come true?

Lya said, "Dear, our cause, to be successful, has to be their cause. They must believe in the principles on which Shangri-La has been built. True to Shangri-La's principles, nothing can be or should be forced upon anyone. They will embrace our principles only if they understand where they come from, the foundation on which they stand, that is Life itself. It is the most valuable possession of humankind and all the flora and fauna." Ryan nodded in agreement," Your words are so true, my love. We have to tread the ground very gently. At every step we need to show respect for their ways. And yet, they themselves realize that certain things are simply not working anymore and they are looking for ways to fix them. Also many of the problems which other countries are facing are global. They do not stop at national boundaries. They affect even Shangri-La. My love, perhaps the more we talk about our cause, the more we can find ways to be able to serve their cause. I am beginning to see the possibilities. It is beginning to look like we have to define our mission, set up clear goals, deliberate on them objectively and define ways to make them happen". Lya replied, "Yes dear, I also feel the same way. Bit by bit things are beginning to fall in place. And very importantly, I feel that together we can fulfill our mission".

They were quite happy with their search for defining their mission. It was beginning to take shape in their minds. To do it together gave a new feeling to both of them. Lya began to see Ryan now more as a partner than as a student. Ryan, as before, respected Lya's calm wisdom and was secretly delighted to provide "assist" to her thinking. It was time to celebrate. They headed for the dining car and presently enjoyed their well-deserved meal, over a glass of wine.

The train rolled on. Their minds were filled with anticipation about their new life. While they devoted most of their minds and conversation toward the greater cause of making more Shangri-Las happen throughout the world, another chain of thought was demanding a lot of their attention too. Not really a thought, but a sort of a dream about their new life as a married couple. Ryan was hesitant about bringing it up. "My love, what kind of a home would you want?" Lya always admired Ryan's sensitive approach. But she wanted to be playful and answered, "Why, you still can have your room at the inn. And I already have mine. And we will meet in the evenings and weekends as before." Ryan replied, "You are being naughty. I cannot live at the inn forever. The inn-keeper will throw me out. And now, I don't have my RV even. I shall have to have a home away from the inn. And since I cannot live away from my beloved Lya, the case is pretty well closed. Won't you say so?" Lya merely blushed and said nothing. They continued with their sweet nothings.

The train pulled into Nondon Central Station, located near Shangri-La Plaza. Maya and Leon received them with beaming faces. They embraced both Lya and Ryan. Maya showed her emotions: ”Son, down deep I knew that your love for our daughter would win the day. Since you left, she was not herself anymore. Even though she was carrying on with her work as diligently as ever, something was terribly missing. We could see it on her face and counting days for your return. Welcome back, son, welcome home.” Ryan embraced them both. Tears of joy rolled down Lya’s cheeks.

They took an electric bus to Inn Jasmine. Ryan was happy to get his room back. Lya joined her parents as before.

●

Chapter 18. The New Home and Workplace

Lya's parents proceeded with making arrangements for the wedding. Ryan proposed that the event would take place on the cruise in the evening on River Padma, where he had proposed to Lya and she had accepted his proposal albeit with a caveat, that her parents would have to approve it. The idea of taking the same cruise was so romantic that it appealed to everyone. Ryan's parents and siblings came and stayed at Inn Jasmine. Lya invited her neighbors, her colleagues and childhood friends, with whom she grew up and played even hide-and-seek. The couple took the vow in front of a very learned and well-respected senior, who conducted the ceremony and explained the meaning of every word of the vow, and of marriage and its lifetime implications. He explained eloquently to the couple as well as those gathered for the occasion that marriage is for the couple's entire lives, come whatever may, and that it was also a union between two families. A vow was a promise in front of all present that must not be broken under any circumstances, no more than one could break the bond with one's parents, children and siblings. This last part of his explanation had great significance in view of the prevalence of "no-fault divorce" and "turn-style" marriage" in many countries and their virtual absence in Shangri-La. There were almost no broken homes there and no children, whose lives would be devastated through a broken home. He ended his explanation by saying, "Enough of my serious talk. This evening, we are here to celebrate the union of two wonderful human beings. They have a noble mission in their life together. I feel that they are truly up to it. Let us rejoice." All present made a toast to the beaming couple. Gentle music filled the spring air.

Ryan and Lya had bought a small row-house on a small landscaped courtyard near Inn Jasmine. It was a two-storey building with a complete apartment upstairs and a large open space on the main floor to function initially as their workplace, and if ever it was needed, as an apartment for Lya's aged parents. They decided that they would maintain their life somewhat as an extension of their "getting-to-know-you" stage, during which they met mostly in the evenings and weekends and did a lot of outings. The two young people thought that it would be rather romantic to give each other little surprises and have some new experiences every day if possible. Nondon and all of Shangri-La provided endless opportunities if one really sought them out. And they decided to find them. Lya would continue with her work at the Ministry of Well-Being, since she felt that her being at the Ministry would keep her up to date with its goals, policies and implementations and would help her tie in their mission with the National Service for mutual benefit. Ryan being more knowledgeable about the developed and developing countries, which he had visited extensively during his nomadic period of life, would be better suited to give shape to their mission of making more Shangri-Las come into being.

They furnished their apartment upstairs in the traditional Shangri-Lan style, complete with floor-to-floor mats and sparse furniture to include a traditional hidden-in-wall pull-down bed, a low-rise table and lots of cushions. They had a nice view of the courtyard in front and a tiny vegetable garden in the rear of their house. The apartment had its entrance from both the courtyard as well as from the workspace below, by way of a narrow staircase. The workspace was however furnished like a typical workshop with several computer stations, a projection wall and a small glass-enclosed conference room. It had a mezzanine, which served as a resource center with storage for essential printed matters and supplies. It was accessed by a spiral staircase. Ryan was mighty pleased with his fixing up the place to their own plans. He consulted Lya at every step and was the first to admit that her refined taste for forms, textures and colors had no match. Lya was secretly very pleased with the enthusiasm with which Ryan was literally making Nondon his home. What more could she and her parents expect? Once their home was ready, they invited her parents and a few close friends to visit, which they did most happily. There was a small celebration with some snacks, sweets and wine. They left merrily in late evening. With that Lya's and Ryan's new life began as a newly-married couple.

Next morning Lya woke up with a gentle nudge from Ryan, who stood by the side of the bed with a tray bearing two cups of steaming hot tea. Lya could not believe her eyes. Seeing her surprised look Ryan coyly remarked, "You see, years of living in a RV has made an early-riser out of me and I also taught myself to make tea expertly and what's more, almost any and all dishes using one single recipe. Lya laughed. She told him, "Now, I am going to teach you to make all kinds of delicious vegetarian dishes, using lots of different recipes and you will be able to cook to your heart's content." Ryan pretended to be alarmed and replied, "No, my love. You know how clumsy I am. My cooking would be a disaster. But I promise to prepare the early-morning tea and the breakfast, since those are not complicated." They would have frequent plays with words as they tried to adjust to their new roles, while doing all they could to help each other with all household chores and to take care of each other in earnest.

Amidst all the excitement about setting up their very own household, they had not forgotten their parents, in particular Lya's parents, who were used to having their beloved daughter at Inn Jasmine. In fact one of the reasons for their buying a home near the inn was to make sure that Lya's parents remain in the orbit of their new life quite prominently. In all this Shangri-Lans were quite mindful of their responsibilities toward their elderly parents. Lya continued to spend some time during the weekends at Inn Jasmine helping her parents with receiving guests as she had received Ryan one day and with their book-keeping. And they had already thought of accommodating her parents if need be in old age. As for Ryan, he made a habit of visiting his parents in Freedomland as often as possible and keeping in touch with them at all times through the electronic media. It was not ideal but the best he could do nevertheless. He also made it a point to invite them and his siblings to visit them at any time and for special occasions, like it was for their wedding.

●

Chapter 19. Visit to the Ministry of Global Relations

Now that their life as a married couple was beginning to look less and less like a mere dream and in fact more like a dream come true, Ryan and Lya felt that they must search for ways to make their other dream, that of seeing other countries embrace what made Shangri-La a country in which well-being of all of its citizens had been achieved, also come true. They decided that the first step would be for Ryan to meet the Minister of Global Relations. Because of his genuine interest in learning about Shangri-La, Ryan was a familiar figure to most of the Ministers at the National Service. As such, he could get an appointment with the Minister readily.

He had not met her before. Sheila, the Minister, was a most amicable lady in her fifties. The Ministry was housed in a modest two-storey building facing Shangri-La Plaza, It had a carefully thought-out circular inner courtyard with a large pool of water, on which floated a huge glass globe, portraying the map of the world. The transparency brought the world together both visually and symbolically. Around the courtyard there was a continuous mural depicting the moments of glory of each continent. A beautifully designed trellis formed a dome over the pool. A portion of the enclosing building was open to both the courtyard and an exterior garden.

Ryan arrived on time and was received by the Minister warmly. Over tea Ryan explained to her about the mission of Lya and himself and presented her with a copy of his book, ”Shangri-La. It’s Real”. She paged through the book intently and when she was finished complimented Ryan heartily and responded to his mission quite positively. She said, “Ryan, it so happens that one of the goals of our Well-Being and Happiness Council of the National Service has been to assist other countries embrace our way of measuring development and progress in terms of Gross National Well-Being or GNW as opposed to Gross National Product or GDP. It is no accident that this Ministry is called the Ministry of Global Relations. We genuinely believe that we are a part of a global family of nations. We do not feel that the two words, "foreign affairs" are conducive to that sense. Hence this Ministry is named The Ministry of Global Relations. Anyway, going back to what I was saying earlier, we positively wish to assist. The key word is "assist", like they do while playing a soccer game. The country we assist, must want to have our assistance in the first place." Ryan could not agree more for he knew only too well how proud his own country Freedomland was and how it would resent any overt effort for another country to influence its affairs, even if that made a lot of sense.

The Minister continued, "We are beginning to see some of the global problems which, in the final analysis, have no national boundaries. A few which come to my mind readily are global warming and the rise in ocean levels together leading to increasing violent weather incidences and the most tragic loss of life and property. Shortage of sweet water without which most life on land would perish is growing alarmingly. Pollution of air and water throughout the world resulting in disease and death to all animals including humans continues unabated. Then there is widespread deforestation and desertification. Nations are using up mineral resources at a breakneck speed while ironically weeping over what future holds for the next generations. Some are concerned about their rising debts while ironically hoping for ever-greater consumption to come to their rescue. While the GDPs of certain nations are rising rapidly, so is the globally widening gap between the rich and the poor. Ryan, we can go on, for the list is endless. The point is that many countries are beginning to be aware of the global problems, which would affect them sooner or later. They are also intensely aware of the shortcoming of using GDP as the measurement of development, since GDP misses out largely on the intangibles, which are the essence of Life. Herein we can assist other nations." Ryan thought that he had heard similar sentiments from his beloved Lya too. He was impressed with the fact that the leadership of Shangri-La was so much in tune with the essence of what matters most and that instead of getting mired in the complex web of the symptoms it always focuses on the causes.

Ryan already had a proposal in his mind. He had discussed it with Lya earlier during several of their recent outings. Now came the real test of their proposal. He felt that he was not going to have too many opportunities like the one he was having right now. But he did not wish to overstep his boundaries at the same time. Somewhat hesitantly he got out his message, “Sheila, I would like to know how you feel about letting responsive, or shall I say, potentially responsive nations know that we would like to assist them, if, only if, they would like to have our assistance?” Sheila enthusiastically responded, ”Of course, that is exactly what I would like to do. We have to find a way to do it. Ryan, you have studied this land and had a good opportunity to view Freedomland objectively too and perhaps in your mind compared the two many times over. How best can we achieve our objective of assisting other nations in a realistic manner, while using our resources optimally?”

Ryan and Lya had already thought about it. He replied, ”Perhaps we could organize a global conference here in Nondon on the subject of Gross National Well-Being. Instead of suggesting outright that it is the most comprehensive way to measure the development of a nation, we could make it the subject of discussion.” Sheila responded, ”Absolutely. It is a marvelous idea. Since many countries are already searching for ways to come up with an alternative measure at best or a supplementary one at the least, for a nation’s development, we should get a good response. Let us do it. Since you are so dedicated to the cause and have already devoted so much of your time and other resources to serve it, it will be my pleasure to appoint you as the First Coordinator for the global conference. I am also well aware of Lya’s keen interest in the matter too and her depth of knowledge and great wisdom. If you wish to be joint coordinators I shall be only too happy to propose it, however since she is working for the Ministry of Well-Being, it may be too strenuous for her to be involved in a second major role at the same time."

For Ryan it was like a second dream come true, almost that is. Lya was her first dream and would always remain so. What the Minister said was almost beyond his expectations, since, until recently he was a mere stranger to Shangri-La. How could he ever imagine that he would be asked by the Minister of Global Relations to coordinate a conference that could potentially change the outlook of the world? The immensity of the task started to weigh on him already. As he regained his composure, he said to the Minister most humbly, "Sheila, I am honored by your very considerate offer. It will be my greatest pleasure to be of service to the country that has made me one of its own. I shall of course discuss it with Lya and if you will allow me would like to meet you again soon." Sheila gave an understanding look and agreed to meet him soon again. With his palms folded, he took leave of the Minister.

After Lya returned home in late afternoon, her face beamed with happiness at the sight of Ryan, who rushed forward and embraced her. After a few moments he said gently, "I must share some good news with you, but after you have taken a well-deserved rest, my love." Since Lya already knew what Ryan was trying to do, she could not hide her excitement. She said, "I knew that the Minister would be charmed by this young-man, whom I adore. So, it is a 'yes'. Am I right, my dear?" Ryan replied, "How can my beloved be ever wrong? I did put forth our proposal to organize a global conference to Sheila and she not only liked the idea but wanted us to coordinate it jointly. Wouldn't that be a most exciting project for us?" Lya replied promptly, "My dear, I chose you as my life-partner because of my highest faith in your abilities to not only make me the happiest person on earth, but to take care of lesser tasks like organizing a global conference well too. I shall be by your side at all times, but I want so much that you prove yourself to Shangri-La your real worth. I want you to do it alone because I love you beyond words." Ryan was stunned by her reply and merely said, "My love, you never fail to surprise me with your selfless gifts to me. How fortunate I am to have you as my life's partner! I shall try my best to live up to your expectations. But, promise that you will continue to show me the way as you have since I met you." Lya merely touched his hand as if to reassure him that she would.

A few days later Ryan met with the Minister of Global Relations again and let her know that he alone would coordinate and Lya would help him by being by his side. Sheila was not surprised. Lya's reaction was just what she had expected and she felt happy about it. She knew that when the time came Lya would take up a role that the country needed her to take. For now, Sheila proceeded with the next step, and that was to ask Ryan to come up with a plan of action. She reminded Ryan that she expected that time and resources would be used optimally, in keeping with the country's philosophy to neither maximize and also nor minimize necessarily. Ryan had already discussed the issue with Lya. He told Sheila,

”My initial thinking is that we would involve our students in a major way in this mission. After all it is their world of future to which we are trying to give a more positive shape. The process itself could help build bridges between Shangri-La and other countries and would remove any sense of imposition.” Sheila liked what she had heard thus far and said, ”Ryan, I am with your chain of thought. Lya has done a remarkable job of putting you in tune with our approach to problem-solving. Of course what we are talking about now is not a problem. It is an opportunity. Please tell me how I can be of help.”

Ryan replied, ”If you will allow me I would like to formulate my plans more clearly. I can promise you that I shall have a long list to present to you.” Sheila was amused that Ryan did not share his wish list readily and admired his intelligent step, vis-à-vis his wish list. She merely said, “So be it. But let me have it soon. ”An overjoyed Ryan took leave if her respectfully.

●

Chapter 20. First Thing First: Lya's Participation

Even though Ryan had accepted Lya's wish that he did it alone without her, emotionally he felt lost without her being by his side as always. Unlike before, he needed the interaction with her to keep him going. He decided that he simply needed her badly enough to come up with a plan to just make it happen without giving her a chance to bow out.

After a few days he met with the Minister of Global Relations a third time. By now they felt easy with each other so that formality took a back seat. Sheila greeted him by saying, "What mischief have you cooked up this time?" Ryan was taken aback. Could she possibly read his mind? He replied impishly, "None whatsoever. I just wanted to meet you to present to you my wish list." Sheila, "Well?" Ryan, "Sheila, I have been thinking that I am not an employee of the National Service, which has got to be the face for the global conference. Yet we will have to invite and interact with the governments of other countries. Sheila, as much as I am dedicated to the cause and feel honored to be chosen as the coordinator of the global conference, I cannot possibly represent our National Service to other governments. You might agree that instead of me we could better have someone else who was already well conversant with the entire concept of Gross National Well-Being to officially represent us and interact with other governments." Sheila peered at Ryan through her gold-framed glasses and interrupted him, "Aha. Could we by any chance be thinking of the same person to do the job?" Ryan visibly turned red in face. He knew that the Minister saw it right through. He replied very briefly, "I think, yes." Sheila replied, "That is not going to be any problem. I can request the Minister of Well-Being to transfer Lya to this Ministry till the conference is over."

Sheila asked a visibly beaming but embarrassed Ryan, "And now, what are your other wishes?" "Not too much more than what we have already discussed the other day. I request your help to involve students from all over the country and possibly also a good many number of students from other participating countries in our project, the global conference. I feel that it would be a good way to utilize our resources and time. I shall appreciate it if you arrange for me a meeting with the Minister of Human Resources Development." Sheila replied, "That is eminently sensible. It will be my pleasure to do so. And what else? " "Thank you for asking. I shall need some help in producing visual presentations. Perhaps the Universities and their Schools would already be equipped to do so and in that case we will not have to spend additional funds." Ryan added, "I cannot think of anything else at this very moment. If I may, I would request that a rain check be granted at this time. I shall not forget to optimize at every step." Sheila replied, "I have the confidence that you will. The rain check is granted. I shall personally contact the Minister of Human Resources Development and let you know about your meeting with him." Ryan took leave of the Minister with folded palms.

When he saw Lya in late afternoon, he could hardly hold back his excitement. “My love, you won’t believe it. Something very interesting happened during my meeting with the Minister of Global Relations. As we were discussing the tasks involved in the global conference, she pointed out that we would need someone to represent the National Service to make contacts with the governments of other countries, someone who knew the principles behind Gross National Well-Being extremely well. And she proposed your name as that someone. Also, she said that she would request for your temporary transfer to her Ministry just to be our official spokesperson to the representatives of other governments.” Lya knew Ryan only too well and could easily see through his mischievous ploy to get her involved without going back on his promise. She merely said, ”Aha. And you want me to believe that you did not play a role in helping her with her selection?” Ryan would not lie. He replied, “My love. Honestly, as much as I wanted to, I did not explicitly suggest your name. It was she and she alone who did it. But I cannot tell you how happy I am with her choice. Frankly, darling, I just could not bear the thought of going it alone. This way, we will both be involved, you will walk with me every step but our roles will remain essentially separate. Most importantly, true to your wish, I shall coordinate the project alone, while feeling your touch along the way, like in the old times." Lya merely said, "You are just crazy. But I love you all the same."

With Lya's participation assured, Ryan sensed in himself a new bout of energy and enthusiasm. Even Lya, though she truly wanted to present her beloved Ryan to Shangri-La for what he was, was herself beginning to feel the pain of being a bit removed from his work. She was happy to be able to participate without diminishing his role at all. There was a new burst of energy in her.

Ryan, in his mind, decided that the proposed global conference would be holistic and would include not merely selected issues like global warming or financial systems which could not solve all the problems in isolation, but all issues concerning the well-being of humanity. He pondered over the challenge of covering all issues and came to the conclusion that instead of being torn apart by so much, he would have to focus on the mother of all issues and let other issues be generated from there. This was exactly the entire philosophy of Shangri-La, as taught so patiently by his beloved Lya.

Lya , in the meantime, received a call from the Minister of Well-Being Andre, requesting her to meet him. She had already known the purpose of the call. Nevertheless, as she was one of the most dedicated and knowledgeable of his people, Andre felt that he must let her know in person. Over tea, he made it very clear that her transfer was only till the conference's work was complete. After that she would return to his Ministry and resume her role of policy formulation, in which, as the Minister even said, she excelled.

Ryan and Lya met in late afternoon and decided to celebrate their joint involvement in the project. But they did not wish to talk about the project. Instead, they just wanted to be with each other and feel reassured of each other's presence. They took their favorite cruise boat on River Padma, as they often did and spent the evening just being the happily married couple. They had a candle-light dinner, listened to the soft music being played on the boat and talked just sweet nothings. As they rode back to their home on their electric bicycles, they just felt each other's heart and did not wish to take away that very special feeling with words. The sky was bright and the silence of the night was beautiful.

●

Chapter 21. Ryan meets the Minister for Human Resources Development

The Minister of Global Relations had already set up an appointment for Ryan to meet with Ramon, the Minister of Human Resources Development. When at the due time Ryan met this very distinguished-looking man, what impressed him most was his face, a face which shone as if with the glow of wisdom. Ryan thought how appropriate that was for the position he was holding. Ramon received him most warmly. Ryan presented him with a copy of his book, ”Shangri-La. It's Real”. Ramon told him that he had already read the book and was impressed and moved by its contents and more so, since it was written by one who had come to Shangri-La only as a stranger. He also informed Ryan that he had already been briefed by Sheila about the reason for Ryan's visit.

Like most buildings housing the Ministries, the one for Human Resources was also designed to convey a sense of the theme of the Ministry itself, that being Humans as a vital resource. It also had a courtyard with a lush almost forest-like garden in the middle as if to remind all of the roots of human beings. The surrounding high walls depicted very eloquently the uniqueness of Life in the entire endless Universe and human progress through the ages, starting with the times when they were mere hunter-gatherers to their gradually moving away almost completely from their roots in favor of technology. They showed how the sense of dignity of human scale in all spheres of life was being eroded to the detriment of people's health and sense of oneness with their environment. While waiting to see the Minister, Ryan walked around and absorbed as much as he could. He was fascinated and looked forward to seeing more in the future.

Ramon invited him to have tea first, as was customary. He enquired, "How can I be of assistance to you?" Ryan told him, "I would like to involve our students, particularly the University professors and students in this project of ours, namely, organizing a global conference about Gross National Well-Being.

Toward that I respectfully seek your permission to contact the First Professors of the various universities in Shangri-La and seek out their help." Ramon replied, "Would you need all the University professors and students though?" Ryan politely answered, "Possibly not. In fact only the final year students of Well-Being and their professors would be enough most probably. In my enthusiasm I was being a bit hasty in thinking of involving all the students, even though that perhaps would be ideal for such a momentous conference. I do know First Professor Ava of the National State University. But I do not know yet how many students are there in the various disciplines. With your permission, I could meet her again and find out more." Ramon answered, "Of course. But, you could find the number of graduating students in Well-Being in the entire country on-line. I advise you to do so and determine how many universities you would need to involve. It will be my pleasure to inform the First Professors accordingly. But, since you know Ava already, I shall inform her right away that you will raid her University soon." Ryan replied, "I very much appreciate your gesture."

Ramon was curious about how Ryan intended to use the talents of the professors and the students. He asked, "Ryan, what do you have on your mind about the way you would utilize these talents?" Ryan replied, "They are well-versed with the concept and practice of well-being and they would obviously know the ramifications of GNW being used as the measure of development of Shangri-La or any country for that matter, as different from GDP or gross national product in most other countries. So, I am thinking of asking them to help me with preparing audio-visual presentation materials, including one or more documentary films, to make the case for GNW and what it really stands for. I simply cannot do it alone. I shall however work with them at all times and provide them with guidance as needed. Hopefully, my book "Shangri-La. It's Real" can be a good starting point." Ramon was quite pleased with Ryan's response and felt that the professors and students would have a great experience and that they would be quite proud of their achievement. He said, "Ryan, I am with you. Count me in if I can be of any help as your project develops further." Pleased with the Minister's reaction, Ryan thanked him profusely and took leave of him.

While making the initial contacts, Ryan had been thinking in his mind what could be an appropriate name for the conference. He toyed with different ideas in his mind. It should be expressive yet not too pompous. How about "World Conference on Well-Being?" Would that sound like a conference on health? Or, could it be "Conference: GNW One?" Nope, it sounds too curt and too technical. Could it be "Conference on Happiness and Well-Being?" Or, "World Conference on Happiness and Well-Being?" But those sounded like happiness and well-being were two separate things. To us, Shangri-Lans, the two embraced each other and became an inseparable one. Ryan gravitated toward a straightforward "World Conference One: Gross National Well-Being", which, he felt was expressive, not too technical and made it very clear that there would be more conferences in the future. He decided that he would discuss this with Lya and would also seek the approval of the Minister of Global Relations.

As he met Lya in late afternoon, as usual during weekdays, he embraced her gently and confessed, "My love, I miss you all the time." Lya replied, "That's good. I don't want you to forget me while you get more and more absorbed in your project .Now please tell me how have you fared with Ramon?" Ryan replied, "Well, he is a very wise man. He immediately saw through the excesses in my plans to engage all the university students in the country. Of course in Shangri-La optimum is the rule. So, I have scaled back to the idea of involving only the graduating students of Well-Being." Lya replied, "Thank you, my dear. Now, I can involve all the junior students to help me with my work to reach out to the representatives of other governments and take care of them when they are here." Ryan, "Quick thinking. That is pure Lya. Now, I have to tell you something that I have not told even Sheila, the Minister of Global Relations." Lya, "Tell me the secret." Ryan replied in all seriousness, “My love, I need you to help me make the final selection of what we name our conference. I have, in my mind, thought of several alternatives.” He proceeded with his alternative names and stopped at “World Conference One: Gross National Well-Being” and looked at Lya expectantly. She knew that look only too well. “That’s the one. I like that one most, I love it.” Lya said excitedly. They always played these little games. Ryan drew her near and whispered, ”You win. I want you to win always.”

Together Lya and Ryan met Sheila, the Minister of Global Relations, the very next day and informed her of the plans about naming the conference. Sheila liked the fact that Ryan observed the courtesy of informing her and said, “Ryan, you are the First Coordinator of the conference. It is only fitting that you select its name. I take it for granted that you have already discussed it with your lovely wife. Besides, I like the name. I wouldn’t change it one bit. Tell me where do we go from here?” Ryan told her about his meeting with Ramon and that he would now take the crucial step of meeting with the First Professor Ava, then meet with the professors of Well-Being and get on with the preparation of the presentation materials for the conference in earnest. Having received her approval of their proposals, they respectfully took leave of Sheila.

The two came out of the Ministry jubilant. All were going well and they were together. Lya enquired with Ryan, “Dear, have you decided which countries to invite and how to invite?” Ryan, ”No, my love. That is a most delicate task. We should be able to identify those countries which are already trying on their own to find alternative ways. But even there presently economists and bankers are calling the shots. Data and indices still rule for anything and everything. In their way of thinking the all-important intangibles seem to have no place. That has to change. I have a great deal of respect for them and we will include them too but not exclusively. Hopefully we will find a noted economist who is open to including the intangibles in his or her calculations. And we will invite philosophers and ecologists too. What do you think my love?

When we meet the professors and students of Well-Being, I like to expound on our thoughts so that we all understand what presentation materials we will have to prepare for the conference. Meanwhile, I wish to rely all the way on my lovely teacher to make the decision regarding whom to invite and how, for she is my greatest friend, guide and philosopher." Lya thought he never failed to amaze me, crazy as he was. She said, "You are as always being very naughty. You are shifting the burden on my shoulders. Alright let us do it truly jointly. We will invite noted scholars from diverse disciplines as keynote speakers. And we will invite countries which are already seeking an alternative to GDP but we cannot specify whom they should delegate to the conference. That brings up the question of how we can at least influence their choice. We are also left with the question of persuading the hard-and-fast followers of GDP as the measure of their countries' development to open their minds to GNW. I was wondering if we could solve all these issues simultaneously."

Ryan never could stop admiring the thought process of this very special lady. He replied, “Surely my love. The process that comes to my mind is that we could draw up an agenda for the conference, an agenda devoted to explaining the all-important index to measure human well-being, its “how-s and why-s” and send it to the heads of the governments of selected countries along with the invitation to delegate their representatives. That would leave it to the head of a state to decide who he or she considers it appropriate to delegate. Depending on the number of governments which respond positively, we may have the very distinguished representative of Shangri-La’s National Service pay a visit to the individual countries.” Lya took Ryan’s last proposal in stride and replied, ”My dear, visiting so many countries would be a very strenuous and time-consuming job. Besides, I know someone who would feel very lonely, if this representative stays away from Nondon so frequently. So that part of your plan is respectfully negated, except perhaps to invite a few very eminent persons to give the keynote talks."

Lya continues, "Dear, what can we or should we do to attract or invite countries, which are adamant about using GDP as the measure of their progress? " Ryan replied, "Since this is going to be the first world conference on Gross National Well-Being, we may be wise to limit ourselves to those countries which are already looking for an alternative. My reading is that number by itself would be quite sizeable. Perhaps we could use our experience with the first one to plan beyond. What do you say, my love?" Lya replied mischievously, "That's quite a concession from your earlier plan to delegate poor me to visit so many countries, I must say. But seriously, what you are saying is very wise. As the saying goes, we must make haste slowly. So dear, can we call it a day and have a meal at one of the food stalls at Shangri-La Plaza?" Ryan felt embarrassed that in his zeal for the project, he neglected to think of his dear wife's most immediate need. He replied, "Of course Darling. Why didn't I think of that earlier? Let's do it." They walked hand in hand in silence, as they often did as if to feel each other's heart.

●

Chapter 22. Briefing the Team

Armed with all the necessary approvals, Ryan wanted to proceed with the actual preparation for the conference, which was going to be called "World Conference One: Gross National Well-Being." To make it easy for Ava, the First Professor of the State University of Nondon, Ryan and Lya met her together on the following day. She had already been briefed by the Minister of Human Resources, Ramon. She was expecting the two and received them warmly saying, "Lya, I am so happy that you accompanied the stranger. It is so heart-warming to see you together as a happily married couple." Lya blushed. Her face was beaming and she remained silent. Ava continued, "Frankly, when I saw Ryan last, I invited him to give a talk at the University. Now I understand that he is preparing to give a talk to a much larger audience, a global audience. And you will be by his side. It is wonderful. Now, tell me, what you both have on your minds." Ryan spoke first," My entire presentation will be to give a voice to what Shangri-La stands for and what this country has been built upon. GNW is its measure. Thanks to you and others and to this daughter of Shangri-La sitting next to me, I have learnt so much and understood well how the whole world could benefit from the same lessons. It was most generous of the Minister of Global Relations to ask me to coordinate the conference." Ava said, "I also understand the very important role your lovely wife has been asked to play. I fully agree with her choices. It will be my pleasure to be of assistance to you two. Go on with what you were trying to explain."

Ryan said, "Ava, I shall need the help of the professors and the graduating students of Well-Being to help me put together a presentation that would not only show the beauty of our system, our principles, our approach to assuring well-being of all, but also where and why other systems fail, if I may say so, based on my intimate knowledge of both. I know well that it's a tall order but I also know that we must aspire high, for the alternative is to settle for less to start with." Ava was stunned by what she had just heard. Even Lya was surprised by the intensity of Ryan's conviction. But she had full faith in his ability to achieve the lofty goal. Ava merely said, "If you can achieve what you are aspiring to do, it will be a contribution of enormous proportions to all humanity. I assure you of my all-out help. And what about you, Lya?"

Lya said, "My role is essentially to play host to the delegates of other countries and local participants. I shall take care of inviting them first. For these tasks I am hoping that I can use the help of the Juniors in Well-Being from this university and if need be from other universities as well. My first task is to prepare an agenda, which would appropriately signify that we do not want to talk about merely economic development but most importantly about the importance of Life, happiness and well-being. We want to attract those delegates who would be willing to discuss both objective and subjective issues."

Ava remarked, "I can see why Ramon would choose our star team. You are absolutely on the right track. Let me call the Professor-in-charge of Well-Being. Her name is Mira. I alerted her already about your intentions in general. She would be expecting you both and would have assembled the other professors and the students of the graduating class. Let me walk you to where they are waiting to meet you." Soon Ryan and Lya found themselves in a well-equipped, well lit and acoustically well-insulated lecture theater with a seating capacity of about two hundred. Mira came forward and greeted them with the customary folded palms. The others stood up to greet the couple, who greeted them in return. Mira introduced them briefly and informed the gathering of the purpose of the meeting.

Ryan did not want to waste any time. He started briefing his team right away. "On behalf of both Lya and myself, I like to thank the Professor-in-charge for her kind introduction. I also like to thank the professors and the graduating class to offer me the opportunity to talk to you. Friends, as you may have known already, we are about to embark on a task of historic proportions. Why historic? Since it has the potential of benefitting countless, yes my friends, countless people from all over the world by simply shifting our emphasis from mere economic development to Life, Well-Being and Happiness. You are the true experts in the field. We need the benefit of your expertise in putting together the presentation materials for our conference, which as you may have been told already, will be called, ”World Conference One: Gross National Well-Being.” The Professor-in-charge has assured me that your work for the conference will be counted towards your degree. I request the professors to form small teams and assign them parts of the work. While hoping that my book ”Shangri-La. It’s Real.” could be of some help in defining the work, I have given ten copies of the book to the School’s library. Any questions, so far?”

One of the students asked, ”Sir, we have some know-how and experience in putting together audio-visual presentations. But ours is not of the highest professional quality. Are we going to reach out to our School of Media Arts or an outside agency for that?" Ryan said, "Excellent question. We certainly want the best of presentation. The answer is, yes. We will first tap our School of Media Arts and in the unlikely event that they cannot do the job, we will reach out to an outside agency. I like to inform you at this point that the Minister of Human Resources Development has made it clear that he would like to practice what we preach. We must optimize our use of resources. I am sure that with your help we can do it. Any other question? "

Another student asked, "Sir, where are we going to hold the conference? Obviously, if we are going to have audio-visual presentations for a global conference, we would require a sizeable and sophisticated venue." "That is another excellent question. Yes, of course, but mind you, our purpose is not entertainment and showing of audio-visuals for special effects. Most importantly, I do not have to worry about it. The Minister put the responsibility of hosting on the shoulders of my wife, who as you probably know works with the National Service. She will also be responsible for preparing the agenda of the conference and inviting delegates of various governments. So, I would rather that she answers your question." Lya said, "You will be happy to learn that we will be allowed to hold this conference of national importance fittingly in the conference facilities of the National Service itself. Naturally, I am very happy about it. However, true to our way of life, we will not restrict ourselves to the confines of the indoor spaces only. We will find ways so that our invitees can see, rather experience, the real Shangri-La. That is how this stranger standing next to me learnt about this country firsthand and fell in love with it." As she spontaneously uttered the last sentence she quickly realized its double meaning and blushed. She recovered quickly and asked, "Do you have any other questions relating to hosting etc.?"

One student asked, "Are we also going to be divided into presentation and hosting teams as mentioned before by Ryan?" Lya replied, "Yes, but not as one set of teams separated from the other set. We want that each team will work for both preparing presentation materials as well as for hosting. This will help coordinate better and also give each student exposure to the entire process. I like to add that once we are past preparing the agenda, our work will shift largely to working out the presentation materials, which in turn will give way to hosting the invitees and so on. All this may sound a bit messy to start with but I can assure you that things will fall into place sooner than you may realize."

Next question was, "When do we start?" Ryan answered, "The best question thus far. And you will love my answer. With this meeting we have just started." Next question: "Then when do we complete our work?" Ryan replied, "Wow! I am amazed by the mature level of questioning. This one is a rather difficult one. So, as I always do with difficult questions, I shall let Lya answer this one." She said," It is a difficult question indeed. Frankly, it depends on several factors, like our agenda, our ability to put together the work within a specific time limit, the availability of the representatives of other governments, the general weather at the time of the conference, your own dates to complete your work for your degree, to name a few. I would hazard a guess that we are talking about three months in the least. A most important fact to remember would be that once we announce a date to other countries we cannot go back on it." Silence followed, till a professor spoke out, "Spring would probably be the best time to hold the conference. We are about to start our Spring Semester, which ends in April. That would give us just about four months. The weather is generally excellent at that time and of course our trees are in full bloom." Ryan said, "Thank you Professor, for finding the right answer to a rather difficult question. Now we know better than ever which way to turn when we are in a bind." Everyone smiled including the professor herself.

Ryan added, "If you all will agree, we have accomplished quite a bit for our inaugural meeting. Let us meet again tomorrow. By then we will all have a chance to consolidate our thoughts and you will have time to form your teams. At this time I like to thank all of you for making it a most fruitful session. Perhaps we can adjourn our meeting at this time."

Ryan and Lya felt good about the progress they had made thus far. Nevertheless they also were feeling the pressure of the enormity of the task they had undertaken. Yet, Lya was highly impressed with Ryan's handling of the meeting and his firm resolve. The feeling was mutual. Ryan was equally impressed with Lya's taking control of things and making progress at her end without being pressured by him or anyone else. They felt a strong bond through trying to accomplish their joint mission.

●

Chapter 23. The Agenda and the Presentations

On the following day, Lya and Ryan met the professors and the students again. This time, Lya took the lead for she realized well that till the agenda was formulated nothing else could move forward. She wanted to share her thoughts with all involved in developing the all-important agenda. She thought that this would be the basis of cooperation.

She said, "My friends, as much as we call our conference "World Conference One: Gross national Well-Being", we need to make it evident to all countries our reasons for wanting to use GNW instead of GDP. It is not just a matter of switching from one type of measure for another. Thus a very important component of our agenda would be the presentation of the entire concept of well-Being and how it affects, nay shape, our lives, our mental and bodily health, our environment, our economy, our production objects and methods, our education system, our defense, our attitude towards our environment and our resources, our services and our sustainability. That is a long list, but to you, our students, this must not be new. The next important component would be to present the short-comings of a system that essentially equates maximization of production with well-being and happiness. In this context, I like to add that a growing number of countries are beginning to accept the evident shortcoming of GDP as a measure of well-being. But unfortunately there are many holdouts. Another component would be to present the developing global problems, which know no boundaries and affect all countries no matter which system one pursues. Beyond these there would be a component which specifically presents and discusses the role of the intangibles in solving national and global problems. Based on these major components of the agenda, we will have to develop a detailed agenda after we hear from our intended guest speakers and invitees and find out their needs. I think I have spoken long enough. Please let me hear from you what you think about the matter of the agenda."

A student asked, "I am curious to learn whom we are inviting to the conference". Lya replied, "I have not finalized a list yet, but we intend to invite specifically those countries which are already looking for a change from using GDP or at least to use GNW in conjunction with GDP. We will also invite a number of well-respected people to be our keynote speakers. Ultimately, the list has to be approved by the Minister of Global Relations. The invitations will go out to the respective Heads of State and to the guest speakers by mail, electronic mail and also through follow-up phone calls. Our agenda is intended to make it eminently clear that ours will be an all-inclusive conference, where the participants will talk about not only the tangibles or measurable but also, extremely importantly, the intangibles, which give Life its true meaning. "

Ryan added, "I like to add regarding the presentation materials that in keeping with the spirit of Shangri-La, and what Lya has just said, our presentations should not give mere data, charts and formulas, but much more importantly the intangibles behind or beyond those. I have learnt that when one picks a rose petal by petal what remains is not a live rose but a skeleton at best. So, my friends, I want you to make Shangri-La's spirit come through your graphics, the sights and sounds, the unspoken words, the subtle hints. Use poetry, use songs if you must as long they touch the sensitive chords in the hearts of the participants. Gross National Well-Being is much more than data, graphs and formulas. It is Life itself. Let us rise up to it."

A student asked, "Ryan, what kind of images are you referring to?" Ryan, "Oh, they could portray very simple things, which we see here so matter-of-factly that we almost do not notice them. To give you an example: you all rose when we entered this hall to show your respect. That is not the way it happens always elsewhere. We could show images of tight-knit low-rise houses with wind turbine and solar panels, the narrow streets with mostly bicycles, the many walks everywhere, our small-scale shops and industrial buildings, the many plazas with food stalls, the possibilities are unlimited. We could also show our universities, our schools, our community centers and our research laboratories and what goes on in there. Just glimpses of life in Shangri-La, which we take for granted and yet you would have a hard time finding elsewhere. We could show graphically and symbolically how our preventive healthcare system, our marriage system, our national service system, our opportunity house system and even our defense system works. These are mere examples. I am speaking off the top of my head. We can do a much better job if we organize our thoughts and our images."

The professors and the students were visibly moved by the rousing words. They understood what was expected of them. They understood where Ryan was leading them to. As for Lya, she was so proud of her former student that she could not help but wipe a tear of joy. She felt that it was so wonderful to be partnering with this man not only in her private life but also in this momentous project. She said, "I have full faith in our abilities to rise to the occasion. Let us get on with the work right away. Let us start with the agenda. Let us divide ourselves into four teams to deal with the four components which I talked about a little earlier. I request the professors to please head the teams and guide them. Ryan and I will assist the members of all four teams in order to link up the works of all the teams."

The teams worked with the kind of energy which comes only with strong motivation. Ryan, Lya and the professors could hardly keep up with them. Before they knew, a detailed and highly workable agenda was ready. Lya excused herself for a visit to Sheila, the Minister of Global Relations, and informed her about her team's choice for invitees and showed her the draft agenda, as a courtesy. Sheila was very pleased and except to suggest a few token changes, as befits a Minister, she approved it all. She enquired, "How is the stranger doing?", obviously referring to Ryan. Lya took the hint and said, "He is proving himself to be more Shangri-Lan than others. Even I did not realize how deeply he understands and has embraced our way of thinking, our way of living." Having said this Lya felt a bit embarrassed and blushed a little.

Sheila noticed that and replied, "My dear Lya, had I not believed in that I would not have selected him to coordinate this all-important project. I appreciate your keeping me informed, but I have full faith in your abilities and his. March ahead full speed. And count me in at all times. "A delighted Lya thanked her and took leave of her respectfully.

Lya's next step was to send the invitations with the help of their professor-student teams. And this was done at a rapid pace. She awaited receiving the responses. The teams were now essentially free to start working on the presentations. But true to their youthful spirit Lya and Ryan decided to take a break, not just for themselves but for their whole group. So, together with their team members, they visited some food shops and rode their electric bicycles to the same national park, where they had a picnic lunch cooked by Lya soon after they had met. The visit brought back fond memories of their getting to know each other days. This time it was the turn of the professors and the students to know them better and they liked what they saw and cherished the privilege of working with them. It was a festive picnic. The entire team felt rejuvenated.

Presentation work started in earnest on the following day. They had not forgotten to invite the University's School of Media Arts. Now they had a professor and two students from that School join each team. They used Lya's guidelines regarding the four components and Ryan's inspiring talk about emphasizing the intangibles side by side with the tangibles, but all in a manner that touches the heart as much as it touches the brain. Toward accomplishing their goal, they left no stone untouched.

In order to present the concept of well-being they fanned out over the entire country and prepared audio-visual recordings of the different aspects of life, including the built and the natural environments as eloquently outlined by Ryan. They conducted interviews with people of different demographic groups and attempted to portray life in action, so as to give the conference participants a feel for the essence of Shangri-La. They also portrayed

Shangri-La's optimum use of resources and its effect on its economy and the environment, belief in prevention as a superior and cost-effective way to health, reliance on raising some of their own food, providing full employment and equitable distribution of wealth as a nation-builder, and the all-important understanding of Life rather than money as the most valuable possession of humankind. They also realized that to make their point they do not have to resort to any animation, stage-setting and the like. Reality was beautiful and amazingly convincing enough.

To portray the shortcomings of reliance of GDP as the measure of well-being they could rely on the reports of the resultant damage that it was causing. Even if a nation's GDP was rising, so were the unsustainable debt burdens, growing inequity between the rich and the poor and the consequent rise in social unrest, maximization of consumption including that of energy, material resources, arable land and more, and consequent rise in air-and-water pollution, breakdown of social cohesion and resultant rise in mental illness and crime. The list was almost endless. It was becoming increasingly clear that maximizing monetary wealth did not maximize happiness, health and well-being. To the contrary. The teams had to tread the ground gently for to do otherwise would be against the principles of Shangri-La. Also co-relating the cause-and-effect aspect beyond doubt might be very difficult. Thus they resorted to using already existing documents which evidenced the leaders of affected countries voicing their own doubts about the efficacy of using GDP as the proxy measure of happiness and well-being. The team would remind the viewers about USA's Declaration of Independence clearly stating that Life, Liberty and the Pursuit of Happiness were three unalienable rights of her citizens. They would also remind them that the apparently simple things like access to clean air, clean water, the right to use one's feet and the health of one's body and mind were crucially important to the well-being of humanity.

In order to depict the developing global problems which knew no boundaries, they would once again rely on audio-visual reports of current affairs. And there was an enormous amount of material available. Sometimes the cause-and-effect relationships were not evident. This enabled disbelievers to come up with oft strange rebuttals. When the latter would be confronted with the effects of carbon emission in only one century, they would deny by saying that global warming is a part of the natural cycle of earth's climate change. When they were confronted with the fact that the earth's resources were limited and even water was getting scarce, they would say, all that talk were scare tactics and the prices of many minerals including petroleum is actually lower than before if one figured in inflation. They would even argue that vast existing resources have not yet been tapped and yet they would in the same breath express their concern for the future generations. Even in the face of many species of animals and plants becoming extinct or being on the verge of extinction, the demand for some did not stop only to satisfy a few people's selfish ego. Once again the list is endless. The teams bravely worked on these issues, knowing well that some of their findings would be contested. However based on what Lya said they believed that most of the invitees would be learned people with a broad view of the global problems.

The last component, which as Lya had said, was global progress to date and the course for future actions, was a most difficult one. Global progress toward fully or completely substituting GDP was reported in the news media, even though most of the efforts came from economists and bankers because of the popular notion that economic development equates with well-being. The irony of it was that an ever-greater number of economists and bankers were beginning to see that GDP could not possibly cover the ground that people tend to think it covers. Global progress toward physical, social, environmental and many other aspects were also few and far between, in spite of the rising voices of many thinkers and activists around the world. More often than not, the required political will to bring about any change was largely lacking. Nevertheless the teams were determined to document whatever progress that had been made and also identify the causes behind the slow progress. This naturally led the teams to hint at possible solutions which could be considered. They proposed that there should be more conferences of the same nature, more exchange of visits between this Shangri-La and future Shangri-Las and other countries toward ever-greater understanding of what Shangri-La stands for, more books and movies on the subject and greater utilization of today's social media.

Work proceeded in full swing. Enthusiasm was very high. What made all this possible was the work that was being done tirelessly by Ryan and Lya alongside the teams. The two proved to be models in management. They did not believe in "All work and no play". Instead they understood fully well that social interaction must be an integral part to be successful in their efforts. So, they made sure to stop for tea and drop everything and to stop for a decent meal. They insisted on taking time off for playing games like soccer, volleyball and the like, taking a walk, riding the bicycle, watching a movie and so on. A very personal touch was added when the two brought trays full of tea and snacks for the teams, when they would work late on their projects, as they often would in their youthful enthusiasm.

No wonder that the work was done ahead of schedule. Meanwhile Lya received almost unanimous positive responses from the prospective keynote speakers and the invited countries and she felt assured that the delegates would be highly qualified to do justice to their expectations. It was a wonderfully satisfying feeling for her. Working closely with Ryan on a project of this magnitude and importance only added to her that feeling. What gave her the greatest pleasure was that she could see in his eyes how happy he was with all this.

●

Chapter 24. World Conference One: Gross National Well-Being

It was a beautiful April day. All systems were ready to go but with the unique Shangri-La flavor. The invitees arrived mostly by electric trains and buses. Only those from very large distances flew in. They were housed in the many inns, dotting the Capital City of Nondon. Trees were in flower all over the city and birds' songs filled the air. There was no air-pollution and no cacophony of cars and other motorized vehicles. Colorful flags of the countries of the invitees were juxtaposed with those of Shangri-La and added a touch of color to Shangri-La Plaza. The entire atmosphere of the city exhibited a sense of festivity combined with dignity.

The conference would last six days. Indoor sessions were interspersed with opportunities for the invitees to soak up a good bit of real Shangri-La by visiting places far and near, mingling with people and contemplating on what was going on in the indoor sessions.

There would be four full-day indoor sessions, one each for the four components outlined by Lya to the teams. The third day would be reserved for visits and most part of the sixth day for a feast and visits. The structuring of the conference was essentially Lya's child, for she recalled that Ryan had opportunities to meet people, visit places and live like a Shangri-Lan. Ryan understood well her thinking and agreed to the format.

As if out of nowhere in particular some protesters showed up. They were infuriated by the conference's implied support for optimization in everything and feared that optimization rather than maximization would choke up business and create high unemployment, interfere with their free-style living including night-life, turn the clock of progress backwards and in general be repressive. They invited themselves upon knowing about the conference through the news media as well as the social media. Since immigration was rather relaxed in Shangri-La and the would-be protesters did not seem to pose any threat to the country's security there was no problem for them to get in. They were about fifty strong. True to the culture of Shangri-La, Lya met them outside the venue of the conference and invited their representative to address the conference for a designated amount of time. She asked them to join everyone else for tea and take seats. The protesters did not expect such treatment. Instead they expected security guards to turn up in force and drive them away. They were surprised that nothing of the sort happened. They felt a bit disarmed. Lya's invitation and her personality made even the hard-core non-believers in Shangri-La's approach rethink a bit.

Lya had invited four keynote speakers, one for each of the four main sessions. She deliberately chose globally recognized and respected scholars from different fields, like History, Philosophy, Ecology, and Economics, while making sure that all the speakers related their own field of knowledge with its relationship to humankind at large. She knew well that she could not satisfy everyone with her choice but felt comfortable that she tried to cover as many broadly defined fields as practicable. She had also invited the Press, which came in full force and would cover the conference intently. Further, the student members of the teams could hardly hold back their enthusiasm for telling the whole world about their project through multiple social media.

The conference duly opened with school-children entering in a candle-lit procession and singing the national anthem and a number of thematic folk songs relating to the life in Shangri-La. This was followed by the Minister of Global Relations' invitation to all the invitees including the protesters, who felt pretty defenseless by now. She gave a brief introduction to all the countries present. Finally she invited the keynote speaker for the first session, a noted Historian, to the stage. The Historian brought out eloquently the lessons of history with particular reference to the rise and fall of great civilizations through the ages. He explained how excesses, be it in consumption or be it in over-extension, injustice to the poor and the oppressed including the women, unwavering faith in military might and the sense of infallibility of mortal souls had brought about the doom of once mightiest empires and along with that uncountable and senseless human suffering. He pointedly noted that unlike in the distant past when problems were limited in their influence to national boundaries and at times neighboring counties or a few countries across the globe, increasingly their influence had a global reach. He hinted at the need for global cooperation toward preventing an individual country's missteps.

Now came Ryan's turn to make the presentation. First, he asked the entire team to come to the stage and introduced each member individually and very proudly, indicating his affection for and oneness with them. The last one was a beaming Lya, whom he introduced as the teacher who most patiently taught him all about Shangri-La. He also referred to his two sets of proud parents who were occupying seats in the front row as those who carefully and affectionately guided him during his and Lya's formative years in the two respective countries.

The Historian's eloquent talk served as the appropriate background for Ryan's well-prepared audio-visual presentation of the essence of what Shangri-La believed in and how it had given a gentle form to that concept in all aspects of Life and why it adopted Gross National Well-Being as the measure of development of the country. He emphasized that it all started with the realization of the uniqueness of Life in the endless Universe and hence its incomparable value to humanity and all flora and fauna. He showed many graphs and charts but also relied heavily on images of the way of life in Shangri-La. He understood well the saying that a picture is worth a thousand words. The audience was spell-bound with the quality and content of the presentation. They were impressed that it addressed to their hearts as well as their minds. There was almost pin-drop silence as he ended his talk.

Lya deliberately let the representative of the protester group speak next to Ryan. He made the best-case scenario for retaining GDP and felt that with ever-developing sophisticated technology all of global problems could be solved in the future. He talked about drilling deeper and deeper into the earth's crust, mining the moon and the asteroids and colonizing the moon and Mars. He did not have a solution for the ever-expanding population of the earth, but to be fair no one at the conference did, except to go the route of Shangri-La to minimize the effect of resource depletion. His talk was given a patient hearing and his message was included in the discussions which followed in the afternoon session.

The invitees and all the participants adjourned for lunch. To optimize costs and to help the small businesses, the invitees had their lunch at their respective inns. They could also freshen up and rest if they so desired. Even though they found the changing of shoes at the entrance to the inn and again at the entrance to the common bathroom, and not having high furniture in their rooms and instead having mats and pull-down beds a bit strange, they took it all in stride almost as an adventure. The same had happened to Ryan when he had come to the country for the first time. But the seemingly strange systems grew on him when he began to realize their value for cleanliness and optimization.

The conference resumed in the afternoon with one of the professors of Well-Being acting as the coordinator. Discussions, with questions and answers from the floor, followed. Many echoed their own feelings of the lessons of human history. It was recognized that "History (does) repeat itself" and as such no country, not even today's seemingly invincible ones are immune to the consequences of over indulgence in any form. There was unanimity behind the feeling that extreme stances have no place in human progress. All the same some cautioned against going from the extreme of maximization to the other extreme of minimization. The coordinating professor pointed out that in his presentation Ryan had quite clearly advocated optimization of consumption but incidentally he had made a case for minimization when he referred to Shangri-La's use of nano-technology. Ryan's presentation received much praise. There was much admiration for its innovative approach and team-work. As the conference ended for the day, all present including very importantly the protesters, felt that they inched closer to the all-inclusive concept of GNW and the reasons behind it. Quite a few openly praised the agenda prepared by Lya along with the teams and its innovative touches.

The invitees were informed about the many small eating places all over Nondon and the availability of buses to go to any place of their choice. Even though some of them were a bit surprised to learn that there was no conventional night-life, they thoroughly enjoyed the intimacy of the small restaurants inside the many plazas. Taking advantage of the excellent weather, they mostly chose to sit outdoors and enjoy their meals with a glass of wine. Not being served more than one glass and having vegetarian food, even though absolutely delicious, took a bit of getting used to. But down deep they realized that it was for their benefit only. The indoor theater at Shagri-La Plaza showed selected films from the countries represented at the conference. Some went there after having their dinner. Altogether it was a new perhaps a bit sobering kind of experience and they generally liked it.

The second day of the conference started on the following day. The Minister of Well-Being, Mira, whom Lya requested to be the coordinator for this day, welcomed the delegates and all others back. She reminded all that on this day the shortcomings of using GDP to measure well-being and happiness would be the main focus. At Lya's request and in the spirit of Shangri-La's tolerance and hospitality, Mira even invited the leader of the protest group to speak on this day too for a designated amount of time. Now she introduced the day's keynote speaker, a noted Economist.

The Economist first outlined the definition of GDP or Gross Domestic Product as a measure of the market value of a country's gross domestic products, including all goods and services produced. He explained that it had become synonymous with the economic well-being of a country. So far so good. He explained that progressively to many people GDP erroneously rose to the elevated status of becoming synonymous with the measure of general well-being of the people of the country. He did not hesitate to point out that extreme commercialism and the glorification of maximizing production at all costs, even when benefits were not evident, led to this strange situation. Speaking of costs, neither did he hesitate to mention that maximum consumption is causing depletion of the finite resources of the earth, poisoning of two of the most essential life-sustaining commodities namely air and water, rapid deforestation and denudation of hills and mountains, desertification, extinction of animal species, which could presage our own extinction as well since we are a part of the eco-system and more. He pointed out that GDP ignores these and other costs, such as suffering owing to disease, wars, demeaning of women and almost all intangibles, which did matter nevertheless. As he spoke, his voice almost choked up in emotion. He continued that it is well-known that beyond a certain optimum level of consumption, higher levels of so-called wealth not only does not bring happiness but may also cause multiple social, environmental and health problems.

Such words coming from an Economist of his stature left the audience stunned. Sensing this he went on to say that Economists were increasingly being perceived as most insensitive. In reality they were doing their job well. Their task, so far as the interpretation of GDP was concerned, was being done well, even though GDP as a measure of even economic progress alone had its share of shortcomings. But the real culprit was the tendency among some to portray economic well-being as the measure of general well-being and happiness. Whereas that could be true only up to a point, even that argument lost its validity when there were severe disparities between the wealth of the rich and of the poor, since extreme wealth or the lack of it tended to cause distress and finally social unrest.

Speaking next the leader of the protest group contended that the senior Economist did not take into consideration the aspirations of the youth, for whom any talk of slowing down spelled disaster. They did not understand why they, and for that matter developing countries, would be asked to make sacrifices to correct the folly of their older generations' unbridled extravagance. They did not understand why they would have to switch from their unbridled exuberant high tech cyberspace life-style for what they perceived as the sedate way of Shangri-La's life-style.

At Lya's request the Minister of Well-Being, Mira, responded briefly. She pointed out that the comments made by the leader of the protest group were understandable. She added that what was happening today, waking up to the effects of excesses of yesteryears was not new in history. What was new however was that unlike in the past when one man had the power to dictate and lead a country to its doom, now there was a road to venting warnings and hold back even from the brink and take the path to recovery. She pointed out that at times one had to take the proverbial "bitter medicine" to prevent or even cure a fatal disease. She agreed that it was not altogether fair to make abrupt changes but felt that gradual changes could be made relatively painlessly, particularly if such change would bring about true well-being and happiness.

The second session of the day commenced after lunch and a period of rest at the inns. Another professor of Well-Being acted as the coordinator. He invited speakers to give short speeches so that many could be heard. Much appreciation was expressed for the talk given by the noted Economist. There was some support for the concerns voiced by the leader of the protest group too. The afternoon session was primarily devoted to measures which would correct the short-comings of GDP. Some even advocated that GNW, while being a broader measure, needed to be quantified. One speaker outlined several ways to measure GNW or wellness. He enumerated them as economic, environmental, physical, mental, workplace, social and political and went on to suggest that each one of them could be measured by conducting direct surveys and statistics of related factors. Another speaker spoke in terms of health, education, housing, transportation, employment, income, marital status and environment and proposed ways to measure each of them.

Lya felt strongly that the notion that GNW needs to be quantified through identifying measurable criteria defeats the spirit behind Shangri-La's approach to the entire issue and leaves out the all-important intangibles. The fact that USA's Declaration of Independence categorically listed as inalienable rights three intangibles, namely, Life, Liberty and Pursuit of Happiness was never lost on her. In her brief speech, she highlighted Shangri-La's entire philosophy of wellness and hence adoption of GNW as the standard of measurement of the country's development and very importantly of happiness of its citizens. She emphasized that it is the tendency of leaving out the intangibles, including life, liberty and happiness, which is at the root of today's misguided over- reliance on data or numbers at the expense of most valuable human wisdom and intuition. She used her favorite example to underline her point: when one takes a rose apart petal by petal to find out what makes a rose a rose, the rose ceases to exist. She said, "We measure Well-Being and Happiness not by attempting to quantify any more than how a physician tries to quantify the degree of pain the patient is suffering. As much as pain is real, so are life, liberty and happiness." She went on to say that the tendency to solve any and all problems by going after the symptoms is bound to fail unless the root cause is looked into and that root cause for all our problems was one and one only. It was human's misplaced value on the mirage of satisfaction through selfish accumulation of "wealth" and associated pleasures, instead of on Life which is truly the most valuable of all possessions. Everyone present seemed to agree with her philosophy, even the group of protesters. Her talk was as if a breath of fresh air. Ryan saw the return of the earlier Lya in her speech and could hardly hide his sense of pride and joy.

The second day's conference ended thus. Like on the earlier day the invitees were ready to leave for dinner. But today a surprise announcement was made that arrangements had been made for each of the invitees to spend the following day with a family in and around Nondon, so that they could get a real feel for the way of life in the country. The idea was the brainchild of Ryan, who reflected on his own experiences of getting to know the people and their way of life. The families were advised in turn to expose their guests to a number of experiences including visits to places of interest of the invitees' choice. The invitees never had such an opportunity when they attended a conference before and were beginning to appreciate the uniquely relaxed ways of their host country and its emphasis on the intangibles.

●

Chapter 25. The Conference Resumes After a Surprise

The invitees took full advantage of the grand gesture. Even the protesters did not know how to react to all this. They were quite impressed by the fact that they were being given a good hearing. Now they were also invited to individual homes. They could not quite fathom the trusting nature of the locals. Before they realized all the invitees were bonding with the local people, who took every pain to make their guests feel at home. They took the guests to the national parks for picnics, the mountains for hiking, the rivers for fishing and boat-rides, the museums for viewing the concept of oneness of all life forms, the schools and their emphasis on learning through using one's own hands, and the community centers which offered multiple facilities including places for contemplation. Finally in the evening the locals took the guests to the neighborhood plazas for dinner, dance and wine and insisted on their spending the night at their homes, with a promise to take them back to the conference center on the following day. True to the habit of the naturally hospitable Shangri-Lans, they would not take a "No" for an answer. Simply stated, the invitees, including the protesters, were overwhelmed.

The conference resumed on the fourth day. The local people kept their promise and the invitees, all a bit wiser about Shangri-La, were at their seats on schedule. Today's deliberations would be about "The Evolving Global Problems". The Minister of Human Resources Development, Ramon, was invited to be the coordinator of the morning session. He introduced a noted Ecologist, who spoke eloquently of problems that the earth, our home planet, the only place that was known to support life, was facing. She said that the economic problems paled by comparison with what she referred to as a human-made threat to life itself. In particular, she touched upon the threats caused by polluting the very life-sustaining air that all living forms needed to breathe and polluting the very water in which life on earth originated and without which life would literally wither away. She expressed her deep concern for the rapid depletion of earth's resources which helped sustain today's lifestyle that was reliant heavily on technology and without which future generations would struggle for survival. She also cautioned against the wanton destruction of all other forms of life which had as much right to live as humans did and whose disappearance would spell doom to the survival of the human species too. She then outlined a number of other possible global threats: the ever-growing human population vis-à-vis the earth's ability to sustain it, the possibility of world-wide cyber-attacks which could paralyze all systems of vital communications and the lurking possibility of a nuclear or chemical war. She added that if the world heeded to the warnings in time and acted most urgently, the threats could be fully or partially averted or rather minimized. She ended her talk by saying that Shangri-La's policy to optimize and valuing Life, Health of Body and Mind and Happiness above all held the key to success for all countries and the world as a whole. The sobering assessment of the global problems left the participants in a somber mood. The last comment, the one relating to Shangri-La touched a sensitive chord in their minds in a highly positive way. No one, not even the protesters could deny the Ecologist's assessments.

The afternoon session of the day was coordinated by another professor of the team. Once again people were requested to make short speeches only which would relate to today's topic. One wondered why there was little effort to generate sustainable energy, which could satisfy the entire world's energy needs without ever having to run out of it and at the same time helping to keep the air and the water of our lovely blue planet clean and avoiding disaster-causing global warming. Another spoke of the need to use and nourish sustainable resources, which in turn sustained themselves with resources like sun, soil and water. A protester even advocated, "Make love, not war." toward solving nuclear and cyber threats and was happy to be heard. The lively session brought out many good ideas and very importantly a feeling of wide support for the cause that humankind must act before it went beyond a tipping point and much concern was shown for the plight of the future generations as a result of the follies of their parents and grandparents.

A relaxed evening followed. Ryan and Lya were missing each other much but put the cause of the world above their personal feelings. Every now and then they would exchange understanding and affectionate glances. Their pride and confidence in each other knew no bounds. Presently they decided to join the guest of honor, the noted Ecologist for dinner at a restaurant on a plaza and found out how impressed she was by Shangri-La's highly eco-sensitive way of life, its sparkling blue star-studded sky and its fragrant refreshing air, all of which were rarities elsewhere.

Next day was the last day of the conference. The topic was "The Role of the Intangibles in Solving National and Global problems". The coordinator was the eminent educator Ava, the First Professor of Nondon State University. She introduced the guest speaker, an eminent Philosopher. The Philosopher added another dimension to the deliberations. He told the audience that after all that is said and done, human destiny was determined not by legislation, rules and regulations, not by data and numbers, not by how much a country produces, not by all that is physical but by the wealth of mind, the unspoken, the feelings and the moral values, all of them were intangible. He brought up the examples of respecting one's parents and taking care of them at old age. He spoke of commitments made in a marriage to a life-long bond like one has for one's parents, siblings, children and grandchildren and decried turn-style marriage and divorce as an expression of lapse of morality and mindless selfishness. He said that optimum consumption was not a question of how much or how little a country produced but one that should be decided by the need of the body and very importantly the mind, by one's innate sensibility toward exploitation of anything for self-satisfaction or depriving others. Altogether the principles on which Shangri-La was based recognized the paramount importance of the value of the intangibles, as eloquently expressed by the words, Life, Liberty, Happiness and Well-Being. He agreed that he could not prove the value of the intangibles in terms of numbers but since all humans had feelings he hoped that they understood. He expounded his theory at length and closed his remarks by saying that even the way in which the conference was being conducted, the way the protesters were given respect and patient hearing, the way all invitees were made literally and deliberately to feel at home, the country's leaning toward vegetarian food without resorting to compulsions, its optimum use of space, renewable energy and more expressed to him, and hopefully to all present, how valuing the intangibles could bring about real value to life. But before he said he would make his closing remarks he sought to make one more remark and said, "I am yet to see a country which practices equality of sexes, races, ethnic groups and religious groups as honestly". The coordinator, Ava, indicated her appreciation of the noted Philosopher's words of great wisdom and remarked that the conference was having an appropriate ending with an appeal to the heart.

During the session after lunch, which was coordinated by a fourth professor, short speeches were welcomed from all present. One protester said that she liked the emphasis on feelings for she would normally get lost with too many numbers and charts. Most participants could not but agree with the Philosopher in that moral standards were beginning to slip and that none of the problems of the world could be fixed by viewing things from limited angles and through intricate numbers. A Statistician commented that there were umpteenth ways to use any set of data, which could then be easily manipulated to justify or negate a point and he agreed that a message directed to the heart would often be most powerful.

Once again the conference ended on a rather thoughtful but happy note. For now it was an evening of reflection over dinner with the many newly-made friends. Lya and Ryan spent the evening mostly with Ava and their Philosopher guest-of-honor and expressed their deep appreciation of his points of view. He in turn congratulated Lya and Ryan for the well thought out agenda and expressed his sincere hope that some countries would adopt GNW, fully or partially and even more importantly abide by the spirit behind the concept.

On the following day there would be a morning session only and its subject would be a discussion of what would ideally follow this conference, so that its findings and message were not lost. The fine weather continued throughout the conference. At Lya's request Sheila, the Minister of Global Relations coordinated this concluding session, as she did the first one. She thanked all the invitees and also the protesters for their participation and told them that even though this was the concluding session of this conference she would like them to visit her country many times again and continue the dialogue that had just begun. She said that the issues presented and discussed at the six day conference would not disappear or be resolved at the end of this one conference. To be meaningful, this must be considered as the beginning of a continuous process toward progress. She went even so far as asking if any country, which was present at the conference would host the next conference, which could take place as early as a year from today.

The delegates of the participating countries voiced their unanimous support for the call of the Minister and all indicated their willingness to host the next conference. That of course presented a dilemma. To make it interesting and fair and square, Lya proposed that the sequencing be made according to the alphabetical order of the names of the countries. It was decided by the delegates that the actual agenda for the subsequent World Conferences on Gross National Well-Being would be determined by the respective host countries. Almost all the countries wanted Ryan and Lya to take their presentation on Gross National Well-Being to their respective countries toward making a case for their easy adoption. Ryan and Lya agreed, however they also wanted to take their presentation to those other countries in which a large percentage of the people were not supportive of the concept. In fact they were acutely aware of the hostility of certain vested interests in some countries, to whom people were essentially consumers of whatever products they would produce to acquire ever-larger money-wealth.

The official part of the conference ended just in time for a festival at the Shangri-La Plaza, organized specifically to enable the invitees to mingle freely with the locals and get a taste of the life at large in Shangri-La. This was not a formal party. Local people were welcome to participate. There were songs by school children, folk-singers and others. There were dances, some formal and others informal. And there were many food-stalls. Lya and Ryan also let themselves immerse in the joyous party. Lya wore a colorful dress and a rose in her hair. Reminiscent of the "old" times, they took a ride on their favorite carousel and like in the "old" times, Ryan felt that he was dancing with the ever-young, ever-vibrant Lya. They were missing each other throughout the conference and now took this opportunity to reconnect. The guests also could not but notice the bond between the two. The feeling was contagious and not a few new romantic relationships blossomed. The participants, including the initially angry protesters, shared the happiness of Shangri-La as they gradually said “adios” to their hosts. By the evening only a few die-hard souls stayed back for a few more days to soak up a bit more of Shangri-La.

●

Chapter 26. Discontent & Peace

Thanks to the instant reach of the news media and the social media the conference received wide publicity world over. Unfortunately for the organizers and the supporters of the conference, the stream of news and the fact that the concept of Gross National Well-Being was apparently gaining ground, some of the vested interests who wanted to hang on to the practice of glorifying Gross National Product began to feel uneasy. However they would not give ground to the new concept.

Even though there was no immediate and direct cause and effect relationship , there were a number of happenings around the world just at about the same time when the conference was going on, which made many wonder if humankind's unrelenting consumption of earth's resources and avoidance of sustainability in development were the best policies to pursue. Blind reliance on Gross Domestic Product or GDP was the symptom of a severe underlying problem.

Many of the countries from around the world were teetering on the brink of collapse as a result of unbridled spending on one hand and accumulation of unimaginable wealth by a limited few on the other, sometimes even using "ponzi" schemes or using information unfairly. Their national debts were sky-high and well beyond their capacity to repay without undertaking drastic measures to curb spending and consumption that had been deliberately encouraged or pushed, obviously irresponsibly. When the day of reckoning came and the already have-nots were asked to tighten their belts further in order to balance the budget and bring back the same cycle of maximization of production and consumption, people revolted. They revolted against grossly unequal distribution of wealth in many places around the world, even in countries where there was no debt problem. There were revolts against undemocratic rules. There were massive protests against violence of all kinds.

Apart from protests there was an alarming rise in several other sets of problems, which too related to excessive consumption, selfishness and valuing of fleeting pleasures. Among them were the prevalence of obesity, drug abuse, possession of assault weapons and senseless killings and even in some countries maintaining disproportionately huge military forces while the masses starved. Then there were the effects of excessive burning of fossil fuels and the resultant global warming, rise in ocean temperature, melting of the earth's ice-caps, erratic violent storms and untold human suffering. Another very sad development was the rise in human trafficking which victimized mostly women and children. Along with the economic and environmental fabric, the social fabric was taking a severe toll as well. Divorce was rampant causing heartrending suffering of the totally innocent victims, the children. The mobility of the elderly was severely curtailed and their only refuse was assisted living or a life in a nursing home. Gone were the days when generations lived together or in close proximity of each other thus enabling stable relationships. The simple pleasure of walking or biking safely was sacrificed to the overwhelming prevalence of automobiles. Excessive use of potentially highly beneficial gadgets often forced people to communicate with machines instead of real people. Human scale was subjugated, as it was beautifully portrayed by great artist, Charlie Chaplin in the film, “Modern Times“.

Ryan had seen the effects in his home country, Freedomland. He remembered well his own sense of alienation there, the result of having much more than all he needed, the emptiness created by his highly privileged and highly materialistic lifestyle. He had also seen the difference in Shangri-La, the joy of having just enough, the joy of being able to walk or riding a bicycle, the joy of eating and drinking optimally, the joy of raising one’s own vegetables using one’s own hands , of making a stranger feel like one’s own family and so much more. He could not figure out why sanity and humane ways would not prevail and decided to persuade as many countries as possible to change their way of thinking toward creating more Shangri-Las. Lya felt in her heart Ryan's pain, his frustrations and decided to do all she could to let him fulfill his mission. Her respect for Ryan's aspirations brought her ever-closer to him. For the two the conference was the start of a long march towards bringing Shangri-Las to the entire world. It could be an uphill battle but they contemplated on history's many examples of success in the face of seemingly formidable obstacles.

They could not wait another year when the next conference was due to take place. Things were happening at a lightening pace. Nations were fighting ailments by going after the symptoms, without bothering to go to the root of the problems. A restless Ryan and his beloved Lya wondered what they could do to awaken people to the deep-rooted solutions, which Shangri-La had adopted quite successfully and painlessly. They conferred with the Minister of Global Relations, Sheila, who was all ears for this remarkable and dedicated couple. She liked their proposal to contact her counter parts in receptive countries to let their graduating students spend a semester in Shangri-La's universities in reciprocation of the Shangri-Lan students spending an equal amount of time in their countries. Sheila agreed that this was the most effective way to bring about change as desired, since she believed that true to the beliefs of Shangri-La nothing works as well as the bond between people. She agreed to work out the process of exchange with the Minister of Human Resources Development, Ramon.

The thought of exchange of students between receptive countries and Shangri-La made them think of the question of other countries. When and who will try to sway those countries away from their steadfast belief in maximizing production at all costs in the mistaken belief that it was the surefire way to achieve well-being and happiness. So far as Ryan was concerned thinking was doing. He decided that the answer to "Who" could only be "Ryan himself" and the answer to "When" was "Right away". But will Lya agree to his plan? He carefully chose the time and place to ask her the question. It was going to be their favorite evening-cruise on River Padma.

As Ryan planned to seek her agreement to his desire to go it alone to some of the countries which might not be warm to their desire to bring about change and was about to speak, Lya put her hand over his and said softly, "Dear, I have a pleasant news for you. You are going to be a father." A beaming Ryan got up from his seat, walked over to her side and embraced her warmly and whispered, "I love you both". He forgot what he wanted to tell Lya earlier. They danced to the music holding each other closely and let silence speak.

Days and then weeks were passing slowly. The couple could not contain their happiness. They shared the news with their parents and close friends. Ryan, like all would-be fathers, would not allow Lya to exert herself in any manner, even though the health advisor told that she should stay moderately active at all times. Nevertheless he made sure to go out for a leisurely walk with his beloved Lya. They talked about the baby and what would be its name. If it was a girl, they would name her "Lara", a name they both liked, after seeing the movie, "Doctor Zhivago" and which took parts of their two names. And if it was a boy, they would name him, "Neil". On the following day they would again dream up new names. While this play with names was going on, Lya could not but notice on Ryan's face something that was troubling him deeply.

Lya confronted him one day, "What is it, my dear? Something is troubling you, I can tell." Ryan, "Nothing, my love. I am the happiest person on earth." Lya replied, "I know that you are the happiest on earth, dear. But I also sense that something is not alright." Ryan could not hold back and said, "My love, you have made a new man out of me. First when you taught me so patiently what Shangri-La meant. And then you put me in the forefront to present Shangri-La to the whole world. Knowing so well what is happening around the world I feel like visiting some of the countries and let them know about what Shangri-La stands for. With the presentation materials on hand, it would be rather easy. But at the same time, I do not feel like being away from you even for a day." Lya replied, "My dear, I have also made a crazy person out of you. There have been other known cases of fatherhood too. You cannot drop everything just to look after your dear Lya. You must go to those other countries, but don't stay away too long. It is best that I continue with my work at the Ministry of Well-Being, now that the conference is over. I promise to be very careful and when you are not here I can stay at Inn Jasmine with my parents."

Ryan could never stop admiring this remarkable person. Her sacrifice for him knew no bounds. He was so overwhelmed with her words that the only answer he could give was to hold her close to him while tears welled up in the eyes of both. But crazy or not, he would not be swayed from his decision to stay close to Lya at this time. He could not however resist something that he had not thought about. Invitations started pouring in from Universities and some highly dedicated foundations in the GDP-oriented countries for Ryan to be their key-note speakers at convocations or major conferences. At the insistence of Lya, who emphasized that it was his duty to respond favorably, he finally relented. Yes, he would respond to the invitations favorably.

He made short visits to the many places which had invited him. His speeches and the audio-visual presentations were greeted with standing ovations everywhere. Many of the Universities honored him with honorary doctorates. His became a household name. The news media and the social media could not have enough of him. Star anchors featured him on their special prime-time programs. Lya felt that her mission of presenting Ryan the stranger to the whole world was becoming ever-more successful. She also knew that if others saw Ryan's faith in Shangri-La and his ardent desire to make other countries see what he had seen in his adopted country, they would become willing to change their ways readily. While her expectations were not fulfilled as quickly as she would like to, the expected awareness became widespread.

Many months had passed. One fine morning a call came from the Global Peace Foundation. Ryan had been selected as the recipient of the most prestigious World Peace Prize for his untiring and sustained effort to bring about real change in the value system used in most countries through gentle means. The Global Peace Foundation would be honored if Ryan would grace the awarding ceremony with the presence of himself and his wife, Lya, who had inspired him in his mission. Lya was in her advanced stage of pregnancy and would not be able to accompany him. Ryan sent a note to the Foundation indicating his grateful acceptance while regretting that his wife would not be able to attend the ceremony.

On the momentous day Ryan graciously accepted the prize and said that the prize money would be given to serve the cause of Peace. He thanked the Foundation for honoring the cause for which he and his team members were working diligently and graciously acknowledged the inspiration that he had received from his wife Lya and the entire country of Shangri-La. He concluded his speech with an appeal to the entire world to gently walk the road to Peace. His talk received a standing ovation accompanied by a seemingly endless applause. His suggestion that change should be brought about gently as opposed to through any revolution or violence touched a sensitive chord. It was most persuasive.

At the end of his speech he was led to the seat of the guest of honor, next to the President of the Foundation. After he took his seat, the President quietly handed over an envelope to him and told him that the message came to his attention through an Express Delivery company so that Ryan would not be disturbed unduly. Ryan hurriedly opened the envelope. There was his beloved Lya's handwritten message: "Two new members of the family have arrived. They as well as their mother are doing well. Lara, Neil and Lya send their love and congratulations. We miss you. Come home soon."

●

Biography of the Author

A. N. 'Shen' Sengupta is an evergreen person, who had exemplary parents, elders and teachers to guide him in his formative years. A globe-trotter, he went for his formal training to some of the most well-renowned schools in the world, including Harvard and MIT. He also took considerable personal interest in many diverse subjects like history, astronomy, anthropology and preventive health-care. He lived in tiny hamlets and mega-cities on one hand, and on the banks of mighty rivers, in deserts and on mountains on the other. 'Shen' has taught at several universities, and designed and planned many a projects including entire towns, in several continents. All in all, he has seen and experienced much, both joyful and painful, thinks a great deal about many issues staring at our faces and wishes to share what little he believes he understands.

Printed in Great Britain
by Amazon.co.uk, Ltd.,
Marston Gate.